FATE'S REGRET

I WISH WE HAD NEVER MET.

AADITYA VERMA

Copyright © Aaditya Verma
All Rights Reserved.

This book has been self-published with all reasonable efforts taken to make the material error-free by the author. No part of this book shall be used, reproduced in any manner whatsoever without written permission from the author, except in the case of brief quotations embodied in critical articles and reviews.

The Author of this book is solely responsible and liable for its content including but not limited to the views, representations, descriptions, statements, information, opinions and references ["Content"]. The Content of this book shall not constitute or be construed or deemed to reflect the opinion or expression of the Publisher or Editor. Neither the Publisher nor Editor endorse or approve the Content of this book or guarantee the reliability, accuracy or completeness of the Content published herein and do not make any representations or warranties of any kind, express or implied, including but not limited to the implied warranties of merchantability, fitness for a particular purpose. The Publisher and Editor shall not be liable whatsoever for any errors, omissions, whether such errors or omissions result from negligence, accident, or any other cause or claims for loss or damages of any kind, including without limitation, indirect or consequential loss or damage arising out of use, inability to use, or about the reliability, accuracy or sufficiency of the information contained in this book.

Made with ♥ on the Notion Press Platform
www.notionpress.com

To the ones who taught me the true meaning of love,
loss, and self-discovery.
To those who walked away, for you have shown me my
strength.
To the ones who stayed, for your support became my
foundation.
And to myself, for having the courage to let go, rise
again, and rewrite my story.

This is for anyone who has ever loved deeply, hurt
badly, and found the courage to heal.
May we all find peace in the lessons that pain brings
and hope in the promise of tomorrow.

"In every ending, there is a beginning."

Contents

Foreword

In the intricate tapestry of life, we often find ourselves lost in the threads of love, heartbreak, and the painful yet necessary journey of self-discovery. **"Fate's Regret: I Wish We Had Never Met"** is a story that delves into the complexities of relationships, the betrayal that cuts deeper than anything else, and the painful process of picking up the pieces of a heart that has been shattered.

This is not just a love story. It is a tale of growth, of learning to stand tall when the world feels like it's crumbling around you. **Dhruv, the protagonist, represents every person who has ever dared to love, only to be met with the harsh reality of betrayal.** His journey is one of strength, resilience, and ultimately, healing. It is the story of a boy who thought he had lost everything but, in the process, found something far more valuable—his own peace, his own worth.

Through this novel, **I invite you to walk with Dhruv through the heartache and the painful lessons life has to offer.** This is a story of letting go and moving forward, of understanding that love isn't always enough, but it doesn't mean it's the end. It's just the beginning of a new chapter—a chapter where you learn to love yourself again.

May this story remind you that you are never truly lost. No matter how dark the road may seem, there's always light waiting for you at the end. And remember, sometimes, we have to walk through the fire to come out

stronger on the other side.

To those who have loved, lost, and rebuilt themselves from the ashes—this book is for you. Let the journey of Dhruv be a testament to your own strength and resilience.

Preface

Love is often depicted as the most beautiful thing in the world—a force that binds people together, elevates their lives, and makes everything seem possible. But what happens when that love is betrayed? What happens when the person you trust the most, the one you give your heart to, turns away from you and leaves you broken? The story of Dhruv in **Fate's Regret: I Wish We Had Never Met** explores this painful reality.

This novel is more than just a recount of heartbreak; it's a deep dive into the emotions and struggles that come with it. It's a reflection on how relationships can change us—sometimes for the better, but often leaving us with scars that take years to heal. The journey of Dhruv is one of painful self-discovery, where he learns that losing someone doesn't mean losing yourself. The lessons learned through betrayal, the process of rebuilding a broken heart, and the realization that life does not end when love does—these are the themes that shape this story.

While the narrative is filled with sorrow and loss, it is also about hope. It is about how we pick ourselves up after a fall, how we find the strength to move forward when we feel completely defeated. It's a journey of healing, learning to let go of the past, and embracing the future, no matter how uncertain it might seem.

This story was born from the belief that every experience, no matter how painful, carries with it a lesson that will shape who we become. **I hope that as you read Dhruv's story, you can find pieces of yourself within it—whether you've experienced betrayal, heartbreak, or simply the complexity of love.** May you walk away from these pages not with sorrow, but with a renewed sense of strength, understanding, and the hope that **no matter how dark the days may seem, there is always a light waiting for us.**

As you begin this journey through Dhruv's eyes, know that this story is not just his. It is a reflection of everyone who has ever loved, lost, and learned to love again.

Acknowledgements

I would like to express my deepest gratitude to the people who have made this journey of writing **Fate's Regret: I Wish We Had Never Met** possible. Without your love, support, and belief in me, this book would not have come to life.

First and foremost, I owe everything to my Mumma, Papa and Bhai. Your unconditional love, guidance, and constant belief in me have been my greatest sources of strength. Through every moment of doubt and every challenge, you've been there to lift me up. You've taught me the true meaning of perseverance and the power of staying true to myself, and for that, I am eternally grateful. This book is as much yours as it is mine.

To my dear family members, thank you for being my unwavering support system. Your encouragement and presence have made every step of this journey possible. I feel blessed to have such a loving and caring family who always have my back, no matter what.

To my friends and the rest of my inner circle, thank you for being there through every high and low, for always being a shoulder to lean on, and for reminding me of my worth when I needed it the most. Your unwavering friendship has been a constant source of strength. The countless late-night talks, advice, and support have helped shape this story in ways that I can never fully express.

This book is a reflection of all of you. It's a tribute to the love, loyalty, and strength that you've shown me throughout this journey. Thank you for believing in me, for pushing me to keep going, and for being there every step of the way.

Lastly, thank you to my readers. I hope you find something of value within these pages, just as I found strength and understanding in writing them. May this book resonate with you and offer the hope and healing that we all need at times.

To my family and friends—thank you for being my everything. Your support means the world to me.

As I sit here, staring at the blank pages of my diary, I can't help but feel the weight of the words I'm about to write. It's funny how writing can sometimes feel like the only way to make sense of things, to find closure when everything else seems so uncertain. This is my story—the story of a boy who thought he had it all, only to lose it in ways he never imagined.

I'm Dhruv Joshi, an 18-year-old son of Viren Joshi (Papa) and Nirmala Joshi (Mumma). I live in Mumbai, a city where dreams are made, but where pain also feels a little bit more real. I've always been the quiet one, the one who observes rather than speaks, the one who hides his feelings behind a mask of calm. But inside, there's been a storm—an ache that I never knew how to express, not even to the people closest to me.

I grew up in a family full of love. Papa, with his calm wisdom and quiet strength, and Mumma, with her warmth and unconditional support, have always been the backbone of my life. Didi, my older sister, has always been the voice of reason, the one who made sure I never strayed too far from the right path. My family has always been there for me, but sometimes even the people who love you the most can't save you from the chaos within.

This is the first time I'm putting pen to paper about the things I've never spoken out loud. About Naira, the girl who made me believe in love, and the betrayal that followed. I've spent too long trying to forget, trying to bury it deep inside, but writing feels like the only way to move forward. The only way to make sense of the mess I've made of my life, the mess she made of it.

I don't know where to begin, or if I even should. But I feel like it's time to finally let go. Maybe this story will help me understand why I fell for someone who wasn't who I thought she was. Maybe it will help me figure out who I really am in the end.

I'm starting this diary with one goal—to tell the truth. To be honest with myself, even if it hurts. And if you're reading this, I hope you understand that sometimes, **the hardest part of life isn't letting go of someone. It's learning to let go of the version of them that we created in our minds.** That's the hardest thing I've ever had to do.

So here I am, Dhruv Joshi, telling my story. The story of my first love, my heartbreak, and the lessons I've learned along the way. I don't know where it'll take me, but I'm ready to write it all down. I need to.

And maybe, just maybe, this will be the first step in finding my peace again.

1
The Encounter

It was a usual evening in Mumbai—busy streets, honking cars, and the kind of noise that you could never escape. The city never slept, and neither did the pressure that seemed to hang in the air. I sat by my window, watching the lights flicker across the skyline, feeling detached from it all. I wasn't sure where I fit into this chaos, but then again, I wasn't sure where I fit anywhere.

I'm Dhruv, a first-year student at a local college. I study literature, and though I love writing, I haven't figured out where it will take me. Right now, I feel like I'm just drifting along, like a leaf caught in the current, hoping to find something solid to hold onto.

I glanced at my phone, and there it was—a message from Vraj, my best friend.

Vraj: "Dude, you coming to Rhea's party tonight or what? Don't be a bore. I'm dragging you along whether you like it or not."

I sighed. Vraj was relentless when it came to dragging me into social situations. I wasn't a party guy. I never really enjoyed the noise and the crowd, but Vraj had a way of convincing me to join in, even if I didn't want to.

"Mumma, I'm not sure if I want to go out tonight," I told her when she came into my room with a tray of snacks.

"Why not, beta?" she asked, her tone light but insistent. "Vraj invited you, right? It'll be good for you to get out and meet people."

"I'm fine here, Mumma. I'm just writing."

She raised an eyebrow. "You've been writing for hours. Go enjoy some time with friends. You're always so wrapped up in your head. Go, it'll be good for you."

I looked back at my phone. Vraj had texted again, and I knew I wouldn't hear the end of it if I didn't show up.

"Fine," I muttered, "I'll go."

Mumma smiled. "Good. Just don't stay out too late, okay?"

I nodded and left the house, knowing I wouldn't hear the end of it if I didn't go.

ᗷᗷᗷ

When we got to Rhea's place, the noise hit me immediately. People were everywhere—laughing, dancing, and talking over one another. It was overwhelming. But Vraj, of course, was already in the middle of the crowd, chatting away like he was born for this.

I found a quiet corner and leaned against the wall, nursing a drink. I wasn't exactly having fun, but at least it was nice to just watch people.

That's when I saw her.

She was standing by the kitchen counter, talking to a group of people. She wasn't like everyone else—she wasn't trying to be the center of attention. She had this calmness about her, and I couldn't help but be drawn to her. Her long hair framed her face, and there was something in the way she moved that made her stand out. I didn't know why, but I felt like I had to go talk to her.

I walked over to her, feeling a bit nervous, but somehow, the words came out.

"Hey, I'm Dhruv," I said, my voice a bit louder than I intended. "I don't think we've met."

She turned to me and smiled. "Naira," she replied, her voice soft but warm. "Nice to meet you, Dhruv."

"Are you enjoying the party?" I asked, trying to keep the conversation going.

She smiled again, but there was something in her eyes that told me she wasn't exactly having the time of her life. "Not really. I'm not much of a party person, but Rhea's a good friend. I couldn't say no."

I chuckled. "Same here. Vraj practically forced me to come."

"Vraj, huh?" she raised an eyebrow. "You know him?"

"Yeah, he's my best friend," I said, glancing over at Vraj, who was laughing with a group of people.

"I can tell," Naira said, smiling. "You seem pretty different from him."

I smiled. "I guess I am. He's the outgoing one, and I'm more... quiet. I write."

Naira's face lit up. "Really? That's awesome! I sing. I'm studying music."

"Music, huh?" I said, intrigued. "That's amazing. I've always thought music and writing were connected in a way. It's about expressing what you feel, right?"

Naira nodded, her expression softening. "Exactly. It's all about the feeling, whether it's through lyrics or melody."

The more we talked, the more I found myself opening up. I wasn't sure what it was about her, but there was something easy about being around her. She understood, in a way that no one else did.

ppp

By the end of the night, the party was winding down, and most people had left. Naira and I found ourselves outside on the balcony, the cool Mumbai breeze hitting our faces.

"You know, Mumbai is different at night," she said, looking out at the skyline. "It feels like the whole city is awake, but it's peaceful, in a way."

I nodded. "Yeah. It's like everything slows down."

She turned to me then, her gaze meeting mine. "I'm really glad we met tonight. I didn't expect to have such a real conversation."

I smiled, a bit surprised by how much I'd opened up to her. "Yeah, me too. It's not often I connect with someone like this."

She gave me a small smile, and for a moment, the noise from the party and the city seemed to fade. It was just us, standing there, talking about everything and nothing at the same time.

Before we said goodbye, she gave me a soft smile. "Let's do this again sometime, Dhruv. I'd love to hear more of your stories."

I watched her leave, feeling a sense of excitement. There was something about her—something that made me feel seen in a way I hadn't in a long time. As I walked back home that night, I couldn't stop thinking about the conversation, the connection.

ppp

Back in my room, I sat by my desk, the city lights casting a soft glow in the room. I grabbed my pen and started writing, not really knowing where the story would go, but feeling like I had to write it down. Maybe this was the start of something.

The next day felt like a blur. I couldn't get Naira out of my head. Every small detail from the party replayed in my mind—the way she laughed, the way her eyes seemed to sparkle when she talked about music, how easy it was to talk to her. I hadn't felt like that in a long time. I couldn't remember the last time I connected with someone so easily, so naturally.

I spent the whole day trying to focus on my assignments, but every time I picked up a pen or opened my laptop, my thoughts would wander back to that night. To Naira.

Later in the evening, as I was sitting on my bed and scrolling through social media, I saw a notification. It was a message from her. My heart skipped a beat as I opened it.

Naira: Hey, Dhruv. I just wanted to say that it was really nice meeting you last night. I don't usually talk to people so easily, but you made it feel so comfortable. Thanks for being such a good listener.

My hands shook a little as I typed a response. I didn't want to come across as too eager, but I couldn't help myself. I couldn't wait to talk to her again.

I replied, Hey, Naira. I feel the same way. I don't usually open up to people so quickly either, but I felt like I could talk to you without any pressure. It was nice getting to know you.

I hit send and stared at the screen for a moment, waiting for her reply. The minutes felt like hours.

Then, my phone buzzed again.

Naira: Well, I'm glad we're on the same page. So, tell me, Dhruv, what kind of writing do you do? What inspires you?

I smiled, excited that she was interested in what I did. Writing wasn't something I talked about often, especially with people who didn't understand it. But with Naira, it felt different.

I write short stories mostly. I find inspiration in everything around me—in the things people say, in the moments we don't always notice. I guess I'm always observing. I don't know if that makes sense, but it's how I see the world, I texted back.

I felt a sense of calm wash over me as I read her response.

Naira: That makes perfect sense. I feel the same way about music. There's so much emotion in the world, and music lets me express it. I think that's why I connect so much with your writing. It's raw and real.

I felt my chest tighten. She understood. It wasn't just small talk. She truly understood.

I'd love to hear more about your music sometime. Maybe you could sing for me? I asked.

I laughed nervously as I sent the message, wondering if it was too forward. But I wanted to hear her sing. I wanted to know more about the person who had already started to fill so much of my thoughts.

A few minutes passed, and I thought maybe she hadn't seen the message. But then my phone buzzed again.

Naira: I'd like that. I'll send you something soon. But only if you promise to keep writing. I think your stories have a lot of potential.

Her words hit me like a wave. It wasn't just about her singing or about her wanting to hear my stories—it was about us sharing something, something bigger than just casual conversation. It felt like we were beginning to understand each other in ways that I hadn't expected.

I put my phone down, staring out the window at the Mumbai skyline, my mind racing. I had no idea where this was going, but for the first time in a long time, I didn't feel the need to have all the answers.

I was just... living in the moment.

ppp

The next day at college, I couldn't stop thinking about Naira. I walked through the crowded corridors, the sounds of students talking and laughing filling the air, but none of it mattered. I was lost in my thoughts, wondering if she was thinking about me too. I tried to focus on my classes, but the thoughts kept swirling in my head like a storm I couldn't control.

That's when I bumped into Vraj.

"Bro, you've been in your head all morning," Vraj said, nudging me with his elbow. "What's going on?"

I looked up at him, forcing a smile. "Nothing. Just tired, I guess."

"Uh-huh," Vraj said, his eyes narrowing. "Tired? Or is it because of a certain someone?"

I raised an eyebrow. "What are you talking about?"

Vraj grinned. "Don't play dumb with me, Dhruv. You've been acting weird ever since the party. Is it Naira?"

I froze. How did he know?

Vraj laughed. "Come on, bro. You think I wouldn't notice? I know you. You're not the type to get excited about anything, but you've been practically glowing since you met her."

I felt my cheeks flush. "I don't know what you're talking about."

"Sure you don't," Vraj teased. "But it's okay. If you like her, just tell her. What's the worst that can happen?"

I sighed. "I don't know, man. What if she doesn't feel the same way?"

Vraj slapped me on the back. "That's the risk, bro. But you'll never know unless you try. And trust me, I've seen the way she looks at you. She's into you, man."

I shook my head, trying to brush off his words, but a part of me couldn't help but wonder if he was right. I wasn't used to this kind of attention. I was used to being the quiet, invisible one. The one who sat in the back of the room and observed. But with Naira, it felt like I was more than just a passive observer. It felt like I mattered.

ppp

That afternoon, I got a message from Naira.

Naira: Hey, Dhruv. I was thinking about what you said the other night. I'd love to share something with you. I recorded a new song, and I think you'll like it. I hope it inspires you.

I didn't even hesitate. I hit the reply button and typed back.

I'm excited to hear it. Send it over whenever you're ready. I'm sure it's amazing, I replied.

A few moments later, my phone buzzed again. She had sent me a voice note.

I pressed play, and as the soft melody filled my ears, I felt like I was being transported into another world. The lyrics were simple but powerful, raw with emotion. Her voice was unlike anything I had ever heard—soft, yet commanding, vulnerable but strong.

By the time the song ended, I was speechless. I didn't know how to respond, but I knew one thing for sure: I had to tell her how much her music meant to me.

That was beautiful, Naira. Honestly, I don't know what to say. Your voice... it's like it speaks directly to the heart. I hope one day I can write something that captures even a fraction of that emotion, I texted back.

I waited for her response, my fingers trembling as I set my phone down on the table. My heart was racing.

I wasn't sure where this was going, but I knew one thing for sure—Naira was no longer just a girl I met at a party. She was someone who had already started to change my life, someone whose music made me feel things I had never felt before.

As I sat there, waiting for her message, I couldn't shake the feeling that this was only the beginning.

ᑭᑭᑭ

2
The Bond Deepens

The days following our conversations felt like a dream, one I wasn't ready to wake up from. Naira and I had settled into a routine. We texted every day, shared songs, stories, and sometimes, just random thoughts about life. It wasn't anything grand, just two people finding comfort in each other's presence, even if it was through a screen.

I remember one evening, sitting on my bed with my laptop open, trying to work on my latest short story. But no matter how hard I tried, my mind kept drifting back to Naira—her laughter, the way she spoke about her love for music, the way she made even the simplest things sound so poetic. I couldn't stop thinking about her.

Suddenly, my phone buzzed. I grabbed it eagerly, hoping it was her.

Naira: Hey, Dhruv. How's the writing coming along?

I smiled. She had this way of checking in, like she genuinely cared about what I was doing. It made me feel... important.

Honestly? Not too great. I've been distracted lately, I replied.

I paused for a moment, deciding to be honest. I didn't want to pretend like everything was fine when it wasn't.

I think it's because I keep thinking about someone. Someone who makes it hard to focus on anything else, I replied again.

There was a pause. I started to wonder if I had said too much, but then my phone buzzed again.

Naira: Someone, huh? Who's the lucky person?

I hesitated. Should I tell her? Should I tell her how much I was thinking about her? I didn't want to scare her off or make things awkward. But I couldn't lie, not when she was the only one who had been on my mind.

I guess you could say that it's you. You're the one I can't stop thinking about, I answered.

I stared at the screen, waiting for her response. My heart was pounding in my chest. This wasn't just some casual conversation anymore. I had just told her how I felt. Would she feel the same way? Or had I just made a huge mistake?

A few minutes passed, and I began to feel like maybe I had pushed things too far. Maybe she didn't feel the same way. Maybe I had read too much into our conversations. But then, my phone buzzed.

Naira: You're really sweet, Dhruv. Honestly, I'm glad you said that. I've been thinking about you too, more than I should, probably. But it's hard to ignore when you feel such a strong connection with someone, right?

My heart soared. She felt the same way. I couldn't believe it. It felt like everything had shifted in that moment.

So, what does this mean? I asked.

I typed the question before I even realized what I was doing. It felt a little bold, but I needed to know. Where did we stand?

Naira: I think it means we're both figuring this out. But I'm excited to see where it goes. I really like you, Dhruv. And I think we have something special.

The world seemed to stop in that moment. I couldn't stop smiling, my hands shaking as I read her message again and again. She liked me. And she wasn't just saying it out of politeness. She genuinely felt the same way.

❦❦❦

The next few days passed in a blur. Every time I saw her message, my heart would race. It was like I had just discovered a new world—a world where Naira and I were no longer just two people talking online, but two people who were beginning to share something deeper.

One afternoon, I was sitting at the college cafeteria, eating with Vraj and a few of the guys from class when my phone buzzed again. I picked it up, trying to act casual, but when I saw it was Naira, my face lit up.

Naira: So, I have a question for you. I'm performing at a small gig this weekend. Would you like to come? I'd really love to have you there.

My heart skipped a beat. A gig? She was performing in front of people? I had no idea she did that. I'd always thought of her as just someone who loved music, but this—this was different. This was her sharing a piece of herself with the world.

I didn't even hesitate.

Of course! I wouldn't miss it for the world, I replied immediately.

I didn't care what the guys at the table thought. This wasn't just some casual invitation—it was an opportunity for me to see Naira in a new light. To see her passion, her energy, her real self. I didn't want to miss that.

The guys noticed my grin and exchanged looks. Vraj leaned in with a sly smile.

"Who's got you smiling like an idiot?" he asked, winking.

I looked at him, knowing he had already figured it out. "Naira. She's performing at a gig this weekend, and she invited me."

Vraj raised an eyebrow. "Dude, you're going to see her perform live? That's huge. Are you sure you're ready for that?"

I shrugged, trying to play it cool. "I'm ready. I think it'll be… something."

Vraj chuckled, clearly amused by my nervous excitement. "Alright, bro. Just don't go all nervous wreck on her, okay?"

I rolled my eyes. "Thanks for the advice, man."

ᐅᐅᐅ

The gig night arrived, and I couldn't remember the last time I was this excited. I had seen performers before, but this felt different. This wasn't just a show for me—it was an experience. I was going to see Naira, the person who had become a constant thought in my life, pour her heart into her music. And I was going to be there to witness it.

I arrived at the venue, a cozy little café that had a small stage in the corner. The place was buzzing with energy, a mix of students and music lovers all gathered to hear some live music. I spotted Naira talking to a few of her friends near the stage, and my heart leapt in my chest. She looked amazing—her hair flowing down her shoulders, wearing a simple black top and jeans, but it was the way she carried herself that caught my attention. She was confident, like she belonged there, and yet, when she saw me, she smiled and waved.

I waved back, my heart racing as I made my way over to her.

"You made it!" Naira said, her eyes bright. "I'm so glad you're here."

"I wouldn't miss it," I replied, my voice a little shakier than I intended.

She laughed softly, then gestured to the small crowd gathering around the stage. "It's a small crowd, but I'm nervous anyway. I always get this way before performing."

I nodded, understanding more than she knew. "I'm sure you'll be amazing."

She smiled at me, her expression softening. "Thanks, Dhruv. That means a lot."

I found a seat at the back, the excitement building in my chest. The lights dimmed, and the crowd quieted, all eyes turning to the stage. Naira stepped up to the microphone, her guitar in hand, and the room fell into silence.

Then, the first note rang out.

The sound of her voice, raw and beautiful, filled the air. It was like the world around me disappeared, and all that mattered was the music—her music. She sang with so much passion, her eyes closed, lost in the rhythm. And I was there, witnessing it all. It was like I had found my place in the world.

And in that moment, I knew for sure: Naira was something special. And I had no intention of letting her slip away.

As the song ended, the crowd erupted in applause, but my heart was still racing. She was even more incredible than I had imagined. When she looked over at me from the stage, our eyes met, and I could see the warmth in her smile. I smiled back, feeling something deeper stir within me.

The applause faded as the last note of Naira's song lingered in the air, like a lingering whisper. I couldn't move. My eyes were fixed on her as she set down her guitar, stepping off the stage with grace and confidence. The crowd was still clapping, but it felt like the world had slowed down. I couldn't focus on anything but Naira, the girl who had already become so much more than just someone I met at a party.

The moment she walked off the stage, she spotted me. Her face broke into a wide smile, and for a second, everything felt like it was in slow motion.

"Dhruv!" she called out, walking towards me.

I stood up quickly, suddenly aware of how nervous I was. Was I sweating? Why was my heart racing like this?

"Hey, you were amazing," I said, trying to sound casual, but I knew I wasn't fooling anyone. Not even myself.

She laughed, her voice light and full of joy. "You're just saying that. But thank you. I'm glad you liked it."

"I wasn't just saying it," I replied. "You're incredibly talented, Naira. Your voice... it's something else. It made me forget about everything else for a while."

She seemed taken aback by my honesty, her expression softening as she studied me. "Thanks, Dhruv. That means a lot. I guess I get nervous, even if it's just a small gig. But hearing you say that? It makes it all worth it."

The sincerity in her voice sent a shiver down my spine. I didn't know what to say. I felt like I was falling for her more with each passing second, and the thought of it both thrilled and terrified me. What if I was moving too fast? What if she didn't feel the same way?

I quickly pushed the doubts aside, trying to keep the conversation light. "Well, if that's what your small gigs are like, I can only imagine how great your bigger performances will be."

Naira's eyes sparkled with excitement. "I'm hoping one day I'll get there. It's a slow journey, but I think I'm on the right path."

I nodded, feeling a warmth spread through me. "You definitely are. I can see it."

There was a moment of silence between us, but it wasn't awkward. It felt comfortable. We were both letting the conversation flow naturally, letting it unfold without the pressure of needing to say the perfect thing.

"So, how about you?" Naira asked, breaking the silence. "How's the writing going? Any new stories?"

I smiled at her question, grateful for the change of topic. "Well, I've been struggling a bit. I think I'm overthinking it, to be honest. I get these ideas, but I can't seem to get them down on paper the way I want."

She tilted her head slightly, her eyes thoughtful. "I get that. You know, when I'm struggling with music, I just let it flow. I don't worry about whether it's perfect. Sometimes, it's the imperfections that make it beautiful."

Her words resonated with me in a way I couldn't explain. I'd always been so focused on getting my stories just right, but maybe I was missing the point. Maybe I needed to stop being so hard on myself and just let the words come. Like her music.

"That's actually really good advice," I said, smiling. "Maybe I should try to let go of the perfectionist thing."

She grinned, her eyes lighting up. "It works wonders. Trust me. And, hey, you can always send me your stories if you want some feedback. I'd love to hear what you're working on."

My heart raced at the thought of sharing my work with her. But a part of me felt confident. Maybe it was the way she made me feel—like my work mattered, like I had something valuable to share.

"I think I might just do that," I said, the words coming out more confidently than I expected. "I'd like to hear what you think."

Naira nodded, her smile warm. "I'm looking forward to it. And just so you know, I've got your back. I'm here for you, Dhruv."

Her words sent a rush of warmth through me. It was hard to describe the feeling—like she had just opened up a space for me in her world. And I wasn't about to take that for granted.

ᗑᗑᗑ

The night continued with more performances, and though I wanted to stay and hear every single act, my mind kept drifting back to Naira. She was still talking to her friends, laughing and chatting, but every time I looked over at her, I couldn't help but feel like we shared something that no one else in the room could understand. It wasn't just the music. It was the connection we had built in such a short amount of time.

Eventually, the gig ended, and the crowd started to disperse. I made my way over to Naira, who was standing near the exit, chatting with her friends. When she saw me, her eyes lit up again.

"Hey," I said, feeling the excitement bubbling in my chest. "That was amazing. I'm so glad I came."

She grinned, brushing a lock of hair behind her ear. "Thanks, Dhruv. It really means a lot. You're one of the few people who actually gets what I'm trying to do with my music."

I felt a little flutter in my chest. "You make it easy to get. Your passion shines through everything you do."

She looked at me for a moment, like she was weighing something in her mind. Then, she spoke, her voice quieter now. "You know, I'm glad we met. I didn't expect to click with someone so quickly, but here we are."

I couldn't help but feel my heart skip a beat. She was glad we met. That meant something. It meant more than I could put into words.

"I'm glad too," I said softly. "I never thought I'd meet someone like you. You've really... changed things for me."

She reached out and touched my arm gently, a small, reassuring gesture that felt like the start of something bigger.

"You've changed things for me too, Dhruv," she said. "In a good way."

We stood there for a moment, neither of us saying anything, but it felt like the most meaningful silence. It wasn't uncomfortable. It was just two people standing in the same space, understanding each other without needing words.

"Well, I should get going," she said finally, her voice breaking the silence. "But I'm really glad you came tonight. It meant a lot."

"I'm glad I came too," I replied. "And I'll be looking forward to seeing you perform again."

She smiled. "I'll make sure to let you know the next time I'm performing."

I watched as she waved goodbye to her friends and walked out of the venue. My heart was still racing, and my mind was spinning. I couldn't believe how much had happened in such a short time. In just a few weeks, Naira had become an essential part of my world.

As I walked out of the café, the cool Mumbai night air hit me, but it didn't feel cold. It felt like everything was in its right place. The city seemed alive around me, but it was nothing compared to the way I felt in that moment.

Naira had opened something inside me. And I knew, without a doubt, that this was only the beginning of something I wasn't ready to let go of.

ৡৡৡ

The next few days passed, and I found myself thinking about Naira even more. Every conversation, every message, felt like another step in a journey that I wasn't sure where it would take me, but I was excited to see where it went.

But as the days went by, something started to gnaw at me, something I couldn't shake off. It wasn't about Naira—it was about Vraj.

He had been watching me closely, almost too closely. I wasn't sure if it was because he could sense how deeply I was starting to care for Naira, or if it was because he was trying to figure out if something was going on between us. Either way, it was clear that he was noticing changes in me, and I wasn't sure if that was a good thing or not.

I tried to ignore it, focusing on the excitement of getting to know Naira better, but Vraj's knowing glances and teasing comments kept creeping into my thoughts. And a part of me wondered if he knew more than I was ready to admit.

ᐳᐳᐳ

3
The Connection Strengthens

The days after the gig were a blur of excitement, nerves, and late-night conversations. Naira and I talked more often now, and each conversation felt like another brick in the foundation of something beautiful. She had become a part of my daily routine—a text in the morning, a shared song in the afternoon, and long, meaningful chats late into the night.

It wasn't just about attraction anymore. It was about understanding, about learning who she was and letting her see who I was. And the more I got to know her, the more I realized how special she truly was.

One evening, I was sitting on the balcony of my family's apartment, watching the city lights flicker in the distance. Mumbai had a way of feeling alive even late at night. The air was cooler, carrying the faint sounds of traffic and distant laughter. My phone buzzed, and I picked it up immediately, knowing it was her.

Naira: What's your favorite place in Mumbai?

I thought for a moment, staring out at the city. There were so many places I loved, but only one that really stood out.

I replied, "Marine Drive. There's something about the sound of the waves and the endless stretch of the sea that makes everything feel... lighter. Like all the problems in the world don't matter when you're sitting there."

Her response came quickly.

Naira: I love Marine Drive too! It's like the city's soul, you know? I've spent so many evenings there, just thinking and letting the waves carry my thoughts away.

I smiled at her words. She had a way of describing things that made them feel more vivid, more real.

I replied, "Maybe we should go there together sometime. Just sit by the sea and talk about life."

There was a pause before her next message.

Naira: I'd like that. A lot.

I couldn't help but feel a thrill of excitement. The idea of spending time with her in person, away from the noise of the world, felt like something I didn't even know I needed.

ppp

The weekend came, and Naira and I decided to meet at Marine Drive. I was nervous, more than I wanted to admit. It wasn't like we hadn't spent time together before, but this felt different. It felt... significant.

I arrived early, finding a spot near the edge where the waves crashed against the rocks. The sea stretched out endlessly before me, a vast expanse of blue that seemed to mirror the depth of my thoughts.

When she arrived, I almost didn't recognize her at first. She wasn't dressed in the casual clothes I had seen her in before. She wore a simple white kurta with jeans, her hair flowing freely in the breeze. There was something about the way she carried herself—confident yet grounded—that made her impossible to look away from.

"You're early," she said, her voice light and teasing as she sat down beside me.

I answered, "I didn't want to miss even a second of this."

She laughed softly, and the sound was like music to my ears. "You always know what to say, don't you?"

I asked, "Is that a bad thing?"

"Not at all," she replied, her smile widening.

We sat there in comfortable silence for a while, watching the waves crash against the rocks. The city buzzed behind us, but here, it felt like we were in our own little world.

"I come here whenever I need to clear my head," I said finally, breaking the silence. "It's like the sea listens, even when no one else does."

Naira nodded, her gaze fixed on the horizon. "I get that. There's something about the sound of the waves, isn't there? It's like they're telling you that no matter what happens, life goes on."

I looked at her, amazed at how effortlessly she put my feelings into words. "You have a way with words, Naira. It's like you see the world differently."

She turned to me, her eyes soft. "Maybe that's why we get along so well. You see the world differently too. Through your stories, your words. It's like you're painting pictures with your mind."

Her compliment caught me off guard, but I felt a warmth spread through me. "You make it sound like I'm some kind of artist."

"You are," she replied simply. "Even if you don't realize it yet."

ꕥꕥꕥ

As the evening turned into night, the conversation shifted to lighter topics—our favorite movies, embarrassing childhood stories, and the kind of random questions that only two people trying to know each other would ask.

"Okay, your turn," she said, her eyes gleaming with mischief. "What's the most embarrassing thing you've ever done?"

I groaned, leaning back against the stone bench. "Do I really have to answer that?"

"Yes," she said, laughing. "No skipping!"

I sighed, trying to think of something that wouldn't make me sound completely ridiculous. "Fine. There was this time in school when I thought it would be a good idea to impress a girl by reciting a love poem I wrote. Except I forgot the words halfway through and ended up mumbling something about cows and stars. She laughed so hard she nearly fell off her chair."

Naira burst into laughter, clutching her stomach. "Cows and stars? Oh my God, Dhruv! That's amazing. I wish I'd been there to see it."

I replied, "Trust me, you don't. It was horrifying."

Her laughter faded, but the smile remained on her face. "You know, I think that's one of the things I like about you. You're not afraid to laugh at yourself."

I answered, "Well, when you've had as many embarrassing moments as I have, you learn to roll with it."

She looked at me, her expression serious now. "You're one of a kind, Dhruv. Don't ever change that."

Her words hung in the air, heavy with meaning. I didn't know what to say, so I just smiled, hoping it conveyed everything I was feeling.

ϷϷϷ

As we walked back to the main road, I couldn't help but feel like the evening had been perfect. It wasn't just about the place or the conversation—it was about her. Naira had this way of making the world feel brighter, of making even the simplest moments feel special.

"I had a great time tonight," she said as we reached the spot where her cab was waiting.

I replied, "Me too. Thanks for coming."

She smiled, stepping closer. For a moment, I thought she was going to say something, but she hesitated, her gaze dropping to the ground.

"What is it?" I asked gently.

She looked up, her eyes meeting mine. "I just... I'm glad we met, Dhruv. You've made my world a little better."

I felt my chest tighten at her words. "You've done the same for me, Naira. More than you know."

She smiled again, this time softer, and got into the cab. As it drove away, I stood there, watching until the car disappeared into the distance.

As I stood there watching Naira's cab disappear into the chaotic rhythm of Mumbai's streets, the reality of the evening slowly started to settle in. It wasn't just the night that had been perfect—it was her. Everything about her, from her playful laughter to the way she understood the smallest things about me, felt like a puzzle piece sliding effortlessly into place. I couldn't stop replaying her words in my mind: "I'm glad we met, Dhruv. You've made my world a little better."

Those words clung to me like a melody I couldn't forget. As I walked back home, the city felt different. The honking cars, the chatter of street vendors, the sea breeze carrying the scent of salt and earth—everything seemed alive, buzzing with a new kind of energy.

When I reached my building and opened the door to our apartment, I found Mumma sitting on the couch, folding freshly washed clothes. She glanced up at me with a knowing smile.

"You're late today," she said.

I shrugged, trying to keep my face neutral. "Went to Marine Drive with a friend."

"A friend?" she asked, her tone laced with playful curiosity. "Or something more than that?"

"Mumma," I groaned, dropping onto the couch next to her. "It's not what you think. Just a friend."

She raised an eyebrow, her smile growing wider. "You're blushing, Dhruv. Your mumma isn't blind, you know. I've seen this look before."

I sighed, burying my face in my hands. "Fine, maybe I like her. A little."

"A little?" she teased. "It's written all over your face, beta. Whoever she is, she must be special if she's got you smiling like this."

I didn't deny it. How could I? Naira wasn't just special; she was extraordinary.

"Her name's Naira," I admitted softly. "She's... amazing. She's smart, funny, talented. And she gets me, Mumma. Like really gets me."

Mumma nodded thoughtfully, her expression softening. "That's rare, Dhruv. When someone understands you like that, you hold onto them. But remember, love isn't just about the good moments. It's about being there for each other even when things get tough."

Her words stayed with me long after I went to bed. Lying there in the dark, staring at the ceiling, I thought about Naira. About the way she laughed when I told her my embarrassing poem story, the way she looked at the waves as if they held all the answers, the way she had said she was glad we met.

And as sleep finally took over, I found myself wondering what the future would hold for us.

ppp

The next morning, I woke up to the sound of Didi banging on my door.

"Dhruv! Get up! You're going to be late for class!"

I groaned, pulling the blanket over my head. "Five more minutes, Didi!"

"No way," she said, flinging the door open and marching into my room. "If you're late, Mumma's going to blame me. Now get up before I pour water on you."

Reluctantly, I dragged myself out of bed, grumbling under my breath as Didi smirked triumphantly.

"By the way," she said, leaning against the doorframe, "you were smiling in your sleep last night. Who's the lucky girl?"

I froze mid-stretch, glaring at her. "What are you talking about?"

"Oh, come on, Dhruv," she said, rolling her eyes. "I know that look. You've got someone on your mind, don't you?"

I sighed, realizing there was no escaping her teasing. "Her name's Naira. And yes, I like her. A lot. Happy now?"

Didi's face lit up with excitement. "Oho, little brother's in love! This is going to be fun."

"Don't make a big deal out of it," I warned. "It's still new. I don't even know if she feels the same way."

"Trust me," she said, grinning. "If she's smart, she'll see what a great guy you are. Just don't overthink it, okay?"

I nodded, appreciating her advice even if I didn't say it out loud.

ᗞᗞᗞ

At college that day, I met Vraj at our usual spot near the canteen. He was munching on a plate of samosas when he saw me approaching.

"Look who's finally here!" he said, waving me over. "Where were you last night? I tried calling you."

I sat down, grabbing one of his samosas. "Went to Marine Drive with Naira."

Vraj raised an eyebrow, his expression turning sly. "Marine Drive, huh? Sounds romantic."

"It wasn't like that," I said quickly, though I knew he wouldn't believe me.

"Sure, sure," he said, smirking. "So, what's the deal with you two? Are you officially a thing, or are you still in the 'awkward flirting' phase?"

I shook my head, laughing despite myself. "We're just friends, Vraj. For now."

"For now," he repeated, grinning. "I'll take that as a yes."

The conversation shifted to our upcoming assignments, but my mind kept drifting back to Naira. Even Vraj's endless jokes couldn't distract me completely.

ᛈᛈᛈ

That evening, as I sat at my desk trying to work on a new story, my phone buzzed with a message from Naira.

Naira: Hey, what are you doing tomorrow?

I replied, "Nothing much. Why?"

Naira: I was thinking we could hang out. There's this café I love—it's quiet and cozy. Perfect for writing or just talking.

My heart leapt at the invitation.

I answered, "Sounds perfect. What time?"

Naira: How about 4 PM? I'll send you the location.

I replied, "I'll be there."

As I put my phone down, I couldn't help but feel a mix of excitement and nervousness. Spending more time with Naira felt like stepping closer to something I couldn't quite define yet. But whatever it was, I knew I didn't want to let it slip away.

ᛈᛈᛈ

The next day, I arrived at the café early, taking a seat by the window where the sunlight streamed in, casting warm golden hues across the room. Naira arrived a few minutes later, carrying her guitar case.

"Hey," she said, sliding into the seat across from me. "Hope I didn't keep you waiting."

I replied, "Not at all. You're right—this place is perfect."

She smiled, pulling out a notebook from her bag. "I come here whenever I need inspiration. Something about the vibe just works."

We spent the next couple of hours talking, laughing, and even working on our respective passions—her music and my writing. It felt natural, like we had known each other forever.

At one point, she picked up her guitar and played a soft melody, her fingers gliding effortlessly across the strings.

"What do you think?" she asked, her eyes searching mine.

I answered honestly, "It's beautiful. Just like everything you create."

She blushed slightly, looking away. "You always know how to make me feel special, Dhruv."

"You are special, Naira," I said softly. "Don't ever forget that."

Her gaze met mine, and for a moment, the world outside the café faded away. It was just the two of us, two people finding something rare and precious in each other.

As I walked her home that evening, I couldn't shake the feeling that this wasn't just the beginning of a friendship. It was something more—something I wasn't sure I was ready for, but something I knew I couldn't walk away from.

4

The Beginning of Doubts

Days passed, and life continued to flow in its usual chaotic yet comforting rhythm in Mumbai. But something was different. My mind was constantly preoccupied with Naira—her laugh, her little quirks, the way her eyes lit up when she talked about things she loved. Everything about her seemed to have lodged itself into my thoughts, and I couldn't shake it off.

At home, Mumma had started noticing my distracted behavior. One evening, while I was sitting in the living room pretending to watch TV, she came and sat beside me.

"You've been unusually quiet these days," Mumma said, placing a warm hand on my shoulder. "Is everything okay?"

I hesitated for a moment before answering, "Yeah, Mumma. Just a lot on my mind. College stuff."

Mumma gave me a look that told me she wasn't convinced. "College stuff, huh? Or is it something... or someone else?"

I sighed, realizing there was no point hiding it from her. "It's Naira, Mumma. I think... I think I'm falling for her."

Mumma's face softened into a smile. "Love is a beautiful thing, beta. But it's also complicated. Are you sure about your feelings?"

I nodded slowly. "I've never felt this way about anyone before. She's... she's special, Mumma. But sometimes I feel like maybe I'm reading too much into things. What if she doesn't feel the same?"

"Only time will tell, Dhruv," Mumma said gently. "But if your feelings are genuine, you'll find a way to express them. And remember, relationships aren't just about feelings—they're about trust, understanding, and respect."

Her words gave me some clarity, but a part of me still felt restless.

ㄥㄥㄥ

The next day at college, Vraj and I were sitting on the campus lawn, enjoying the rare winter breeze that made Mumbai a little less humid.

"So, what's the latest update on the Naira front?" Vraj asked, lying back on the grass.

I rolled my eyes. "You make it sound like some breaking news story."

"Because it is!" he exclaimed. "Come on, you're hopelessly in love, and I, as your best friend, have the right to know everything."

"There's nothing to know," I said, though my tone betrayed my uncertainty. "We're just friends. She hasn't given me any reason to think otherwise."

Vraj sat up, studying me with an amused expression. "Dude, are you blind? The way she looks at you, the way she laughs at your lame jokes, the way she always finds time for you—it's obvious she likes you."

I wanted to believe him, but doubt lingered. "I don't know, man. What if I'm just imagining things? What if she's like this with everyone?"

Vraj shook his head, patting my shoulder. "Stop overthinking, yaar. Just go with the flow. If it's meant to be, it'll happen."

ppp

That evening, Naira and I had plans to meet at her favorite café again. She had invited me to hear a new song she was working on, and I couldn't say no. When I arrived, she was already there, strumming her guitar and humming softly to herself.

"Hey," I said, taking a seat across from her. "What's the masterpiece today?"

She smiled, setting the guitar aside. "It's still a work in progress, but I wanted you to hear it."

As she played, I couldn't help but admire how effortlessly talented she was. Her voice carried a raw emotion that tugged at something deep inside me.

When she finished, I clapped softly. "That was beautiful, Naira. You've got a gift."

"Thanks, Dhruv," she said, her cheeks turning slightly pink. "It means a lot coming from you."

We spent the rest of the evening talking about everything and nothing—her music, my writing, our dreams, and the little things that made us who we were. But somewhere in the middle of our conversation, I noticed her phone buzzing repeatedly. She glanced at the screen, her expression shifting ever so slightly before she silenced it.

"Everything okay?" I asked casually.

"Yeah," she replied quickly, though her tone was a little off. "Just a friend being annoying."

I didn't push further, but something about her reaction stayed with me.

ᗡᗡᗡ

Over the next few days, I started noticing subtle changes in Naira's behavior. She was still the same warm, cheerful person, but there were moments when she seemed distracted. She'd cancel plans at the last minute or seem preoccupied during our conversations.

One afternoon, I was sitting with Didi in the kitchen while she prepared tea. I decided to share what was on my mind.

"Didi, can I ask you something?"

"Of course," she said, handing me a cup of tea. "What's bothering you?"

"It's about Naira," I admitted. "Lately, she's been... different. I don't know how to explain it, but it feels like she's pulling away."

Didi leaned against the counter, thinking for a moment. "Relationships can be tricky, Dhruv. Sometimes, people have things going on in their lives that they don't know how to share. Have you tried talking to her about it?"

"I don't want to come across as needy or paranoid," I said.

"It's not about being needy," Didi said gently. "It's about being honest. If you care about her, you owe it to yourself to understand what's going on."

Her advice made sense, but I couldn't shake the unease building inside me.

ᕈᕈᕈ

A week later, I finally worked up the courage to ask Naira if everything was okay. We were sitting on a bench at Juhu Beach, watching the waves crash against the shore.

"Naira," I said, breaking the comfortable silence. "Can I ask you something?"

"Of course," she said, turning to face me.

"Is everything okay? You've seemed... distant lately."

She hesitated, looking out at the ocean. "It's nothing, Dhruv. Just some personal stuff I'm dealing with. Nothing to worry about."

I wanted to believe her, but her words felt rehearsed, like she was holding something back.

"If you ever want to talk about it, I'm here," I said softly.

She smiled faintly. "I know. And I appreciate that."

As we walked back to her place that evening, I couldn't help but feel like something had shifted between us. And for the first time, a seed of doubt was planted in my heart—one that would slowly grow into something I couldn't ignore.

As the days rolled on, I found myself consumed by the little changes in Naira's behavior. It wasn't anything major, but small things began to stand out like cracks in a seemingly perfect picture. The way she avoided eye contact sometimes, the subtle hesitation in her voice when I asked about her day, or how she'd glance at her phone and quickly put it away—it all made me restless.

At home, I tried to distract myself, throwing myself into writing and college work. But even in those moments, my thoughts would drift back to her. I wasn't just falling for Naira anymore; I was already head over heels. Yet, that lingering doubt was like a dark cloud hanging over my feelings.

One evening, Mumma noticed me pacing in the living room, my arms crossed as I mumbled to myself.

"Dhruv, beta," she called out, interrupting my spiral of thoughts. "You've been like this for days. What's going on?"

I sighed, sitting down on the sofa beside her. "Mumma, it's about Naira. I don't know... Something feels off lately. She says everything's fine, but I can't shake the feeling that something's wrong."

Mumma put her hand on mine, her touch warm and grounding. "Relationships are delicate, Dhruv. Sometimes, people go through things they don't know how to share. But if you keep holding this doubt inside, it'll only grow. You need to talk to her openly, beta. Be honest about how you feel."

Her advice echoed what Didi had told me earlier, but it wasn't easy to confront someone you cared about—especially when you feared what their answer might be.

ϼϼϼ

At college, I decided to bring up the topic with Vraj during lunch. We sat under a banyan tree on campus, surrounded by the usual noise of students chattering and vendors selling tea and snacks.

"Vraj," I began, fiddling with the edge of my notebook, "can I ask you something?"

He looked up from his plate of poha, raising an eyebrow. "Of course, yaar. What's up?"

"It's about Naira," I said, hesitating slightly. "I feel like she's pulling away. I don't know if I'm just imagining it, but something feels... different."

Vraj studied me for a moment before responding. "Have you talked to her about it?"

"I tried," I admitted. "She said it's just personal stuff and nothing to worry about, but I don't know... it feels like she's hiding something."

"Look, Dhruv," Vraj said, his tone unusually serious. "Sometimes people need space, even from the ones they care about. But if it's bothering you this much, you owe it to yourself to figure out what's going on. Just don't jump to conclusions, okay? Trust is important."

His words gave me some reassurance, but they also left me with more questions than answers.

ᗡᗡᗡ

A few days later, I decided to take Mumma and Papa's advice seriously and speak openly to Naira. We planned to meet at a small park near her house—a quiet spot where we often sat and talked about everything under the sun.

When I arrived, she was already there, sitting on a bench under a gulmohar tree. Her hair was tied up in a loose bun, and she had that faraway look in her eyes that I'd started noticing more frequently.

"Hey," I said, sitting down beside her. "How are you?"

"I'm okay," she replied, smiling faintly. "You?"

"I've been better," I admitted, deciding not to beat around the bush. "Naira, I need to ask you something."

She turned to me, her expression unreadable. "What is it, Dhruv?"

I took a deep breath, my heart pounding in my chest. "Are we okay? I mean, I feel like... like something's changed between us. You've seemed distant lately, and I don't know if it's just me overthinking or if something's really wrong."

For a moment, she didn't say anything. She looked down at her hands, fiddling with the bracelet she always wore. When she finally spoke, her voice was quiet.

"Dhruv, I didn't mean to make you feel this way," she said. "It's just... I've been dealing with some things—personal stuff. I didn't want to burden you with it."

I reached out, placing a hand on hers. "Naira, you're not a burden. If something's bothering you, I want to help. But you have to let me in."

She nodded slowly, her eyes glistening with unshed tears. "I know. And I'm sorry. I'll try to be more open with you."

Her words eased some of the tension in my chest, but I couldn't shake the feeling that there was more she wasn't telling me.

ᱯᱯᱯ

Over the next week, things seemed to return to normal—at least on the surface. Naira and I spent more time together, and she seemed to make an effort to be more present. But every now and then, I'd catch a flicker of that same distant look in her eyes, and it reminded me that something was still unresolved.

One evening, while we were sitting at her favorite café, I decided to test the waters.

"Naira," I said casually, "have you talked to Vraj recently? I haven't seen him around much these days."

Her reaction was subtle but telling. She stiffened ever so slightly, her smile faltering for a fraction of a second before she regained her composure.

"Not really," she said, avoiding my gaze. "Why do you ask?"

"No reason," I replied, though my mind was racing.

As we continued talking, I couldn't shake the nagging suspicion that something was going on—something involving Vraj.

ᐁᐁᐁ

Later that night, as I lay in bed, staring at the ceiling, the pieces of the puzzle started to come together in my mind. The canceled plans, the secretive behavior, the way she reacted when I mentioned Vraj—it all pointed to something I didn't want to believe.

But deep down, a part of me already knew the truth. And as much as I tried to push it aside, I couldn't escape the sinking feeling that the girl I was falling for might be slipping away from me in ways I couldn't control.

The seed of doubt that had been planted earlier had now taken root, growing into something that I knew I couldn't ignore any longer.

ᐁᐁᐁ

5
The Betrayal

The day I discovered the truth began like any other. Mumbai was its usual bustling self, the streets alive with the sounds of car horns, vendors shouting, and life moving at a relentless pace. I was at home, sitting in my room, working on a new story for my writing assignment. But my thoughts kept drifting back to Naira and the strange tension I had been feeling around her.

Mumma walked into my room, carrying a plate of samosas. "You've been in here all day, beta. At least eat something."

I smiled at her, taking the plate. "Thanks, Mumma. Just trying to finish this story."

She sat down on the edge of my bed, watching me with concern. "You've been looking so stressed lately, Dhruv. Is it still about Naira?"

I hesitated before nodding. "Yeah, Mumma. Something doesn't feel right, but I can't put my finger on it."

Mumma sighed, patting my hand. "Trust your instincts, beta. If something feels wrong, it probably is. But don't let it eat you up inside. Sometimes, the truth comes out when you least expect it."

Her words stayed with me long after she left the room.

ᐅᐅᐅ

That afternoon, I got a call from Vraj. It was the first time he'd reached out in weeks, and I couldn't ignore the sudden knot in my stomach.

"Hey, Vraj," I said, trying to sound casual. "Long time, man. What's up?"

"Hey, Dhruv," he said, his voice unusually hesitant. "Are you free? I need to talk to you about something."

"Sure," I replied, my curiosity piqued. "Where should we meet?"

"Let's meet at the chai stall near college," he suggested.

I agreed, though a part of me already sensed that this wasn't going to be an ordinary conversation.

ᐅᐅᐅ

When I arrived at the chai stall, Vraj was already there, nervously stirring his cup of tea. He looked up when he saw me and gave a small, awkward smile.

"Hey," he said as I sat down across from him.

"Hey," I replied, studying his face. "What's going on? You look... tense."

He took a deep breath, avoiding my eyes. "Dhruv, I don't know how to say this, but... I need to tell you something. It's about Naira."

The mention of her name sent a chill down my spine. "What about her?" I asked, trying to keep my voice steady.

Vraj hesitated, his hands fidgeting with his cup. "I didn't want you to find out like this, but... Naira and I... we've been seeing each other."

His words hit me like a punch to the gut. For a moment, I couldn't breathe, couldn't think. The world around me seemed to blur, the sounds of the bustling street fading into the background.

"What?" I managed to say, my voice barely above a whisper.

"It started a few months ago," Vraj continued, his voice filled with regret. "We didn't mean for it to happen, but... we couldn't stop ourselves. I know it's wrong, Dhruv, and I'm sorry."

I stared at him, my mind racing. "You're sorry? You're sorry?" I repeated, my voice rising. "You were my best friend, Vraj. I trusted you. And Naira... she knew how I felt about her. How could you do this to me?"

"I didn't want to hurt you," he said, his eyes pleading. "But things just... got out of hand. I swear, I didn't plan for this to happen."

I stood up abruptly, the chair scraping loudly against the pavement. "You didn't plan for it? That's your excuse? Do you have any idea what you've done? You've ruined everything, Vraj."

People around us were starting to stare, but I didn't care. I felt betrayed, humiliated, and utterly shattered.

"Dhruv, please," Vraj said, standing up as well. "I didn't mean for you to find out like this. I just... I couldn't keep it from you anymore."

"Congratulations," I said bitterly. "You've successfully destroyed our friendship. I hope it was worth it."

I turned and walked away, my heart pounding in my chest.

ƿƿƿ

That night, I couldn't sleep. My mind replayed the conversation with Vraj over and over again, each word cutting deeper than the last. But the worst part was knowing that Naira had been a part of this betrayal. The girl I thought I loved, the girl I thought I could trust, had been hiding this from me all along.

I couldn't stop myself from going through our old messages, rereading the conversations where she had laughed at my jokes, shared her dreams, and told me I was important to her. Every word now felt like a lie, a cruel joke at my expense.

The next day, I decided I needed answers. I texted Naira, asking her to meet me at the park near her house. She replied quickly, saying she'd be there.

When I arrived, she was already sitting on the bench under the gulmohar tree, looking nervous.

"Hey," she said as I approached.

I didn't waste time on pleasantries. "I know about you and Vraj," I said bluntly.

Her eyes widened, and for a moment, she looked like she might deny it. But then she sighed, looking down at her hands. "I'm sorry, Dhruv," she said softly.

"Sorry?" I said, my voice filled with anger and pain. "That's all you have to say? You were supposed to be my friend, Naira. I trusted you. I cared about you. And this is how you repay me?"

"I didn't mean for this to happen," she said, tears welling up in her eyes. "It just... it just happened."

I laughed bitterly. "It just happened? Is that supposed to make it okay? Do you have any idea what you've done to me?"

"I never wanted to hurt you," she said, her voice trembling. "But things between Vraj and me... they were complicated. We didn't know how to tell you."

"Complicated?" I said, my voice rising. "You think this is complicated? You went behind my back, Naira. You lied to me. And the worst part is, I thought you cared about me. But all this time, you were... you were sleeping with him."

She looked away, her silence confirming the truth I had dreaded.

I shook my head, the weight of her betrayal crashing down on me. "You've destroyed everything, Naira. I hope you and Vraj are happy together, because you've lost me forever."

Without waiting for a response, I turned and walked away, my heart shattered into a million pieces.

ᖾᖾᖾ

That night was the longest of my life. I sat in my room, staring at the walls, the silence suffocating me. Every word Vraj had said, every look Naira gave me, every lie they told—it all replayed in my mind like a broken record. My chest felt heavy, like someone had placed a boulder on it, and my eyes burned with unshed tears. I wanted to scream, to yell at the world for being so cruel. Instead, I buried my face in my hands and let the tears flow.

The sobs started quietly at first, but soon they turned into loud, gut-wrenching cries. I clutched my chest, as if trying to hold my broken heart together, but it was no use. It felt like I had lost everything at once—my best friend, the girl I loved, and my own sense of trust. I felt betrayed, humiliated, and completely alone.

"Why? Why did they do this to me?" I whispered to the empty room. My voice cracked under the weight of my grief. "What did I do to deserve this?"

The room felt too small, too claustrophobic. I stood up, pacing back and forth, my hands shaking. My mind raced with questions that had no answers. How long had this been going on? How could they betray me like this? Did they ever care about me at all?

ᗴᗴᗴ

A soft knock on the door pulled me out of my spiral. It was Didi. "Dhruv? Are you okay?" she called, her voice filled with concern.

I quickly wiped my face, trying to compose myself. "Yeah, Didi. I'm fine," I lied, my voice shaky.

She wasn't convinced. The door creaked open, and she stepped inside, her eyes immediately landing on my tear-streaked face. "Dhruv, what happened?" she asked, walking over to me. "Why are you crying? Did something happen at college?"

I shook my head, unable to speak. My throat felt tight, and the words refused to come out.

"Dhruv, look at me," she said, her tone firm yet gentle. She sat down beside me, placing a hand on my shoulder. "Something has happened. I can see it on your face. Tell me what it is."

Her kindness broke the dam I had been trying to hold back. I broke down again, sobbing uncontrollably. "They… they betrayed me, Didi," I managed to say between sobs. "Naira and Vraj… they lied to me. They… they were together behind my back."

Didi's eyes widened, and for a moment, she was speechless. Then, she pulled me into a tight hug, letting me cry against her shoulder. "Oh, Dhruv," she said softly, stroking my hair. "I'm so sorry, bhai. I can't believe they did this to you."

I clung to her like a lifeline, my cries echoing through the room. "I trusted them, Didi. They were the two people I cared about the most, and they destroyed everything. I don't know what to do. I feel like I've lost everything."

She pulled back slightly, looking me in the eyes. "Listen to me, Dhruv. I know it hurts, and I know it feels like your world is falling apart right now. But you have to stay strong. You can't let this break you."

I shook my head. "I can't, Didi. It's too much. I feel so alone."

"You're not alone," she said firmly. "You have me, and you have Mumma and Papa. They don't know about this, and it's better that way. You know how they are. They'll scold you for falling in love, and it'll only make things worse."

I nodded, knowing she was right. Mumma and Papa were traditional in their thinking. They wouldn't understand, and they'd probably blame me for getting involved in something like this in the first place.

"So, please, Dhruv," Didi continued, her voice gentle. "Stay calm. Don't cry anymore. We'll get through this together, okay? But you have to promise me you won't let this consume you. You're stronger than this."

ᐩᐩᐩ

For the next few days, I isolated myself from everyone. I stopped going to college, stopped answering my phone, and barely ate anything. I stayed in my room, avoiding Mumma and Papa's questions by pretending to be busy with assignments. Didi would check on me now and then, bringing me food and trying to get me to talk, but I couldn't bring myself to say much.

The pain of betrayal was like a constant weight on my chest. I'd wake up in the morning hoping it was all a bad dream, only to be hit with the harsh reality all over again. The memories of Naira's laughter, the moments we shared, and the trust I had placed in her felt like daggers in my heart. And Vraj... the thought of him made my blood boil. How could he, of all people, do this to me?

I started avoiding the world altogether. The idea of facing my classmates, knowing they might find out, was unbearable. I felt like a failure, like someone who had been made a fool of.

One evening, Didi found me sitting by the window, staring blankly at the rain outside. She sat down beside me, her voice soft.

"Dhruv, I know it's hard. I know you're hurting. But this isn't the end. You can't let their betrayal define you."

"I feel empty, Didi," I admitted, my voice hollow. "Like a part of me is missing. They took everything from me—my trust, my happiness, my sense of self."

"They didn't take everything," she said, placing a hand on mine. "You still have your dreams, your talent, and your strength. And most importantly, you still have us. We're here for you, Dhruv. Always."

Her words brought a small flicker of comfort, but the pain was still there, lingering like a shadow I couldn't escape. I knew it would take time to heal, but in that moment, all I could feel was the overwhelming weight of loss and betrayal.

ppp

6
The Void

The days after the betrayal felt like a blur, a haze of emptiness and aching silence. Mumbai's chaotic rhythm continued outside my window, but inside my room, time seemed to stand still. It felt like I was trapped in a bubble of pain, unable to break free. The world moved on, but I was stuck in the past, replaying every moment, every word, and every lie.

I stopped going to college entirely. My books lay untouched on my desk, and my phone stayed switched off. The thought of facing anyone—of pretending to be okay—felt impossible. I couldn't bear the whispers, the knowing looks, or the pity in their eyes.

I spent most of my time lying on my bed, staring at the ceiling. Sleep eluded me; my thoughts refused to rest. Images of Naira and Vraj together haunted me. I imagined their laughter, their stolen glances, their secret meetings. It was like a movie playing on loop in my mind, and I couldn't turn it off.

ᐳᐳᐳ

One evening, Mumma knocked on my door, her voice tinged with concern. "Dhruv, beta, you haven't eaten anything all day. Come out and have dinner with us."

"I'm not hungry, Mumma," I replied, trying to keep my voice steady.

She hesitated before saying, "Okay, but don't skip meals like this. It's not good for your health."

As soon as I heard her footsteps retreating, I buried my face in my pillow, muffling the sobs that threatened to escape. Mumma didn't know what I was going through, and I didn't want her to find out. She and Papa wouldn't understand. They'd scold me for getting involved in something like this, for letting my emotions get the better of me.

Didi, however, wasn't so easily deterred. She walked into my room without knocking, carrying a plate of food.

"Enough is enough, Dhruv," she said firmly, setting the plate down on my desk. "You can't keep doing this to yourself. It's been days. You're not eating, you're not talking to anyone, and you're barely functioning. This isn't healthy."

I sat up, my eyes red and puffy from crying. "What do you want me to do, Didi? Pretend like everything's fine? Act like I'm not completely shattered inside?"

"No, I don't want you to pretend," she said, sitting beside me. "But I do want you to fight back. You can't let this break you, Dhruv. You're stronger than this."

I shook my head, tears streaming down my face. "I'm not strong, Didi. I feel so... empty. Like I've lost a part of myself. They took everything from me—my trust, my happiness, my sense of who I am. I don't even know how to move on."

She placed a hand on my shoulder, her voice softening. "I know it feels like that right now, but this pain won't last forever. I promise. You just need time to heal. And you don't have to do it alone. I'm here for you, Dhruv. Mumma and Papa are here for you, even if they don't know what's going on. You're not as alone as you think."

I looked at her, her words offering a glimmer of hope amidst the darkness. But the weight of my grief still felt insurmountable. "I don't know if I can ever trust anyone again, Didi," I admitted. "Not after this."

"You don't have to decide that now," she said. "Just take it one day at a time. And promise me you'll try to eat something. Please, Dhruv."

I nodded reluctantly, taking a bite of the food she had brought. It felt like a small victory for her, but for me, it was just another reminder of how broken I felt.

❦❦❦

For the next few days, I continued to isolate myself. I avoided calls from friends, ignored messages, and stayed locked in my room. The only person I allowed inside was Didi. She was my anchor, the only one who seemed to understand the depth of my pain.

One afternoon, she found me sitting by the window, staring blankly at the street below. The world outside was alive with activity—kids playing cricket, vendors shouting, cars honking—but I felt completely disconnected from it all.

"Dhruv," she said gently, sitting beside me. "I know you're hurting, but you can't keep hiding like this. It's not healthy. You need to step out, breathe some fresh air, and try to move forward."

"I can't, Didi," I said, my voice barely above a whisper. "Every time I close my eyes, I see them. Every time I think about going back to college, I feel like everyone's going to judge me. I just... I can't face the world right now."

"You don't have to face the whole world at once," she said. "Just take one small step. Go for a walk, talk to someone you trust, or even write about how you're feeling. You're a writer, Dhruv. Use that to your advantage."

Her words stayed with me long after she left the room. Writing had always been my escape, my way of making sense of the chaos in my mind. Maybe it could help me now, too.

ᐅᐅᐅ

That night, I sat at my desk with a pen in hand and a blank notebook in front of me. The words didn't come easily at first, but eventually, I started pouring my heart out onto the pages. I wrote about the pain of betrayal, the weight of loneliness, and the struggle to find meaning in the aftermath. It wasn't much, but it felt like a step—a small, hesitant step toward healing.

As I closed the notebook, I felt a flicker of something I hadn't felt in days—a faint sense of relief. It wasn't much, but it was enough to remind me that maybe, just maybe, I could survive this.

The nights that followed were no easier. I found myself caught in the suffocating grip of my thoughts, replaying every moment, every memory, and every lie. It was like a cruel punishment, as though my mind refused to give me even a moment of peace. I would sit by the window, staring out into the dark Mumbai skyline, the distant honks and murmurs of the city reminding me that life was moving on for everyone—except me.

I thought about Vraj. My best friend, someone I considered a brother, who had stood beside me through every struggle, every laugh, and every secret. His betrayal was like a knife in my back, twisting with every thought. How could he do this? How could he look me in the eye, share my pain, and then betray me so deeply? And Naira... her smile, her voice, her promises—they all felt like cruel jokes now. It wasn't just the love that hurt. It was the trust, the belief that we had something special, something real.

ppp

Didi checked on me constantly. Every morning, she would come into my room, sit beside me, and try to coax me into talking. One morning, she entered with a bowl of poha, placing it on my desk.

"Dhruv, I won't leave until you finish this. You're not eating properly, and it's showing. You're not just hurting yourself—you're hurting us too," she said firmly, her gaze soft but unrelenting.

I looked at her, the concern in her eyes making my chest tighten. "Didi, I don't even feel like eating. I don't feel like doing anything."

She sighed, sitting down on my bed. "I know, Dhruv. I know it feels like the end of the world right now. But you need to pick yourself up. You've always been strong, always been the one who kept going, no matter what. Don't let them take that away from you."

I picked up the bowl reluctantly, taking small bites to satisfy her. "It's not that easy, Didi," I mumbled. "Every time I think about moving on, it feels like... like I'm letting them win. Like I'm admitting that they were right to betray me."

She frowned, shaking her head. "That's not true, Dhruv. Moving on doesn't mean you're letting them win. It means you're choosing yourself over the pain they caused you. It means you're taking back control of your life. Don't give them that power over you."

ppp

Despite her words, the void inside me remained. Days turned into weeks, and I fell into a routine of silence and solitude. I avoided Mumma and Papa as much as possible, fearing their questions. They had started noticing my absence at meals, my disinterest in everything around me.

One evening, Papa called out as I walked past the living room. "Dhruv, come sit with us for a bit. You're always locked up in your room these days."

I froze, my heart pounding. I mumbled something about needing to study and quickly retreated to my room. Once inside, I leaned against the door, my hands trembling. I couldn't let them find out. I couldn't bear their scolding, their disappointment. I already felt like a failure—I didn't need them confirming it.

ᕤᕤᕤ

The only solace I found was in writing. Late at night, when the house was silent, I would sit at my desk, pouring my emotions onto paper. The notebook became my confidant, the one place where I could be honest about my pain. I wrote about the betrayal, the memories that haunted me, and the emptiness that consumed me. Each word felt like a piece of the weight being lifted, even if only slightly.

But even writing had its limits. The nights were still long, and the loneliness was unbearable. Sometimes, I would find myself crying into my pillow, the muffled sobs shaking my body. I couldn't stop the flood of emotions—the anger, the sadness, the despair. It felt like

I was drowning, and no one could pull me out.

ᐅᐅᐅ

One night, Didi caught me in one of those moments. I hadn't heard her come in, and when I looked up, her eyes were filled with tears.

"Dhruv," she whispered, sitting down beside me. "I can't see you like this anymore. It's breaking my heart. Please, talk to me. Let it out."

I shook my head, unable to meet her gaze. "What's the point, Didi? Talking won't change what happened. It won't bring back the trust I lost. It won't make the pain go away."

"But it might help you carry it," she said gently. "You don't have to go through this alone, Dhruv. I'm here for you. I always will be. And even if you don't want to tell me everything, at least promise me you won't give up on yourself."

Her words hit me harder than I expected. I nodded, the lump in my throat making it hard to speak. She stayed with me that night, sitting quietly beside me as I let the tears flow. Her presence was a reminder that I wasn't completely alone, even if it felt that way.

ᐅᐅᐅ

In the following days, I tried to take small steps. I forced myself to eat meals with the family, even though every bite felt heavy. I picked up my books, trying to focus on my studies, but the words blurred on the pages. I even considered going back to college, though the thought of facing Vraj and Naira made my stomach churn.

The pain was still there, raw and unrelenting. But somewhere deep inside, I knew I couldn't stay like this forever. I had to find a way to move forward, to rebuild the pieces of myself that they had shattered. It wouldn't be easy, and it wouldn't be quick, but I owed it to myself to try.

As I stared at the notebook on my desk, I made a decision. I would keep writing, not just for myself but for anyone who had ever felt the way I did. My story wasn't just about pain—it was about survival, about finding strength in the face of betrayal. And maybe, just maybe, it could help someone else find their way out of the darkness too.

ᕼᕼᕼ

7
Facing the Shadows

The days blurred together in a haze of lingering pain and reluctant steps forward. I'd begun to interact more with Mumma, Papa, and Didi, but the emptiness within me hadn't budged. Each day felt like a fight to push through. I knew that I couldn't keep living like a shadow of myself forever. I needed to confront the reality of my situation—to face my fears and the people who had torn my life apart.

One morning, as I sat at the dining table with Didi, trying to force down some breakfast, she spoke up.

"You can't keep avoiding college, Dhruv," she said, breaking the silence.

I didn't look up. "I'm not ready, Didi. I can't face them... or anyone else. Everyone knows by now. They must."

She shook her head. "You're assuming the worst, Dhruv. You have no idea what people know or don't know.

And honestly, it doesn't matter. What matters is that you take back control of your life. You can't keep running away."

Her words stung because I knew they were true. Staying locked in my room wasn't solving anything. If anything, it was making the pain fester.

After a long pause, I sighed. "I'll go tomorrow."

Didi gave me a small smile, one that was more encouraging than celebratory. "Good. Take it one step at a time, okay? You don't have to talk to anyone or explain anything. Just go, attend your classes, and come back. That's all."

◁◁◁

The next morning, I got ready for college after what felt like an eternity. My hands trembled as I combed my hair and slung my bag over my shoulder. Mumma noticed and called out as I was about to leave.

"Beta, have your breakfast before you go."

"I'll eat at the canteen, Mumma," I mumbled, rushing out the door before she could ask more questions.

As I walked to the train station, my heart raced. The thought of seeing Vraj and Naira again made me nauseous. I kept my head down as I boarded the train, hoping to avoid anyone I knew. The bustling sounds of Mumbai—the chatter, the street vendors, the clatter of the train—felt overwhelming.

ᗐᗐᗐ

When I reached the college gates, I froze. Memories of laughter with Vraj and Naira flooded my mind. The three of us used to walk in together, joking and teasing each other. Now, I was alone.

I forced myself to take a deep breath and walked in. I kept my head low, avoiding eye contact with anyone. My classmates greeted me with hesitant nods, their expressions a mix of curiosity and concern. It was clear that rumors had spread, but no one said anything outright.

ᗐᗐᗐ

During the first lecture, I felt Vraj's presence before I even saw him. He entered the classroom with his usual confidence, laughing at something another friend said. My heart clenched as I glanced at him. He looked so carefree, as if nothing had happened—as if he hadn't betrayed me in the worst way possible.

Naira wasn't with him, which was a small relief. I didn't think I could handle seeing both of them together yet.

As the lecture progressed, I tried to focus on the professor's words, but my mind kept wandering. I couldn't shake the memories—the late-night conversations, the promises, the trust I had placed in both of them.

ppp

During lunch, I avoided the canteen and found a quiet corner in the library instead. As I sat there, pretending to read a book, I couldn't help but wonder if I was truly ready to be back. It felt like every corner of the campus held a memory, a reminder of what I had lost.

Just as I was beginning to spiral into my thoughts again, one of my friends, Arjun, found me.

"Dhruv," he said, sitting across from me. "It's good to see you back, man. We were worried about you."

I forced a small smile. "Yeah, I just needed some time."

Arjun hesitated before saying, "I know things have been... rough. But you don't have to go through this alone. We're here for you, you know?"

I nodded, grateful for his words, but unsure of how to respond. The truth was, I didn't know how to let anyone in. The betrayal had made me question everyone's intentions, even those who had never given me a reason to doubt them.

ppp

As the day went on, I tried to keep to myself, avoiding any unnecessary interactions. But as I was walking toward the exit, I heard someone call my name.

"Dhruv, wait!"

I turned to see Vraj jogging toward me, his expression hesitant. My entire body tensed. I didn't want to talk to him, didn't want to hear whatever excuse he had prepared.

"What do you want?" I asked coldly, my voice barely masking the anger bubbling beneath the surface.

He stopped a few feet away, his hands raised in a placating gesture. "I just want to talk. Please, just give me five minutes."

I shook my head. "There's nothing to talk about, Vraj. You made your choice."

"Dhruv, it's not what you think—"

"Don't," I interrupted, my voice rising. "Don't stand there and lie to me again. I trusted you, Vraj. I considered you my brother. And you... you destroyed that. Do you have any idea what you've done to me?"

His face fell, guilt and regret etched into his features. But I couldn't find it in me to care.

"I don't want your apologies, Vraj," I continued, my voice shaking. "I just want you to stay out of my life."

Before he could respond, I turned and walked away, my chest heaving with a mix of anger and heartbreak. It wasn't the closure I wanted, but it was all I could manage.

ᡐᡐᡐ

That night, as I sat by my window, I thought about the encounter. Confronting Vraj had brought up all the pain I had been trying to suppress, but it had also reminded me of my strength. I had faced him, spoken my truth, and walked away. It was a small victory, but it was a step toward reclaiming my life.

I wasn't sure what the future held, but I knew one thing: I wouldn't let them define me. Their betrayal was a part of my story, but it wasn't the whole story. I was more than the pain they had caused, and I was determined to prove that—to myself, if no one else.

The nights were getting quieter, but the silence was deafening. With each passing day, the numbness I had once felt seemed to fade, replaced by a steady ache deep in my chest. At times, it felt like I had forgotten what it was like to smile without a mask or to feel genuinely at peace. The weight of betrayal still hung heavily in the air around me, a constant reminder of what I had lost. But slowly, I was learning to navigate through it. One small step at a time.

ᭀᭀᭀ

The next few days passed by in a blur. I went to college, attended my lectures, and spent time with Arjun, who had become a kind of anchor for me during this time. He didn't ask too many questions. He just kept showing up, sitting with me in the canteen or walking with me after class. It was his quiet companionship that I needed the most. No pressure, no pity, just the comfort of having someone who didn't expect me to be okay.

ᐳᐳᐳ

But even with Arjun's support, I still felt like I was carrying a heavy burden. Every time I saw Vraj in college, something inside me twisted. He acted like nothing had changed, laughing and joking with his friends as if he hadn't completely shattered my world. It wasn't the anger that hurt the most—it was the disbelief. The fact that someone I trusted so completely could do this.

It wasn't just the affair. It wasn't even the physical betrayal. What stung the most was the realization that he hadn't cared enough to consider how this would affect me. How it would affect us. He hadn't cared enough to protect the friendship we'd built over the years.

ᐳᐳᐳ

One afternoon, a few weeks after that uncomfortable confrontation with Vraj, I found myself sitting on the roof of our building, staring out at the city skyline. Mumbai had a way of making you feel small—insignificant against its vastness, yet simultaneously a part of something much bigger. I liked coming up here. It was the one place where I could feel alone, but not lonely. The sounds of the city below, the hum of life, were strangely comforting.

I had my phone in my hand, the screen glowing with a message from Didi. "I know you're struggling. I just want you to know that I'm always here for you. Don't bottle it up, Dhruv. Talk to me when you're ready."

I stared at the message for a few moments, then put my phone down. I had been avoiding her lately. Not because I didn't appreciate her, but because I didn't want to admit to her—or to myself—that I still wasn't okay. I wasn't ready to talk. The pain was too raw, too fresh.

 PPP

Just as I was about to get up, I saw a familiar figure walking toward the rooftop. It was Naira.

My heart skipped a beat. I hadn't seen her since that disastrous day when I found out about her and Vraj. I wasn't sure what to expect, or what she expected from me. But I knew one thing—my feelings for her had shifted in ways I couldn't explain. There was no love left, not for someone who could betray me so completely. But there was still pain. There was still a part of me that had once cared for her so deeply, and that made everything harder.

Naira stopped a few feet away from me, her face tense, her hands fiddling with the straps of her bag.

"Dhruv," she said quietly. "Can we talk?"

I stood up, taking a deep breath. My chest felt tight, and my throat went dry. I didn't want to hear her excuses. I didn't want to listen to her plead for forgiveness. But I couldn't ignore her either. Something about seeing her face—seeing the girl I once thought I would spend my life with—made my heart ache in a way I wasn't ready for.

"What do you want, Naira?" I asked, my voice hoarse.

She flinched at the coldness in my tone but didn't back away. "I... I'm sorry, Dhruv. I don't even know where to start. I messed up. I betrayed you, and I hate myself for it."

I wanted to shut her down, to tell her that nothing she said would change what had happened. But there was a part of me, a part I didn't like, that wanted to hear her out. Maybe it was the same part that still wanted to believe in her, in us.

"I never meant to hurt you," she continued, her eyes searching mine. "It just... happened. And when it did, I was too ashamed to tell you the truth. I didn't know how to face you."

I clenched my fists, trying to keep my composure. "So what? You thought I wouldn't find out? You thought I wouldn't see through the lies? You thought I wouldn't feel the betrayal, Naira?"

She lowered her head, tears welling up in her eyes. "I don't know, Dhruv. I don't know what I was thinking. I just... I couldn't stop myself. It's no excuse, I know. But I am so sorry. You mean a lot to me. I never wanted to hurt you. You're my best friend, Dhruv. And I'm sorry I ruined everything."

The words hung heavy in the air between us. I wanted to shout, to scream at her for what she had done, but instead, all I felt was an overwhelming emptiness. This wasn't the girl I had fallen in love with. This wasn't the girl who had once made me feel like the luckiest guy in the world.

"I don't know what you expect from me, Naira," I said, my voice breaking despite my efforts to remain calm. "I can't just forget. I can't just pretend it didn't happen."

She nodded, wiping her tears. "I know, Dhruv. I'm not asking you to forgive me. I just... I needed you to know that I'm sorry. And that I regret everything."

I didn't respond. I couldn't. There was nothing left to say. The silence that followed was heavy, thick with the weight of all that had transpired.

I turned away, walking toward the door. "Goodbye, Naira."

She didn't try to stop me. She didn't say anything else.

ррр

The next few days were no better. If anything, they were worse. My heart was torn in two, and no matter how hard I tried, I couldn't put the pieces back together. Every time I saw Vraj or Naira, the pain came rushing back. I couldn't escape it. It felt like I was suffocating under the weight of it all. But there was no choice. I had to keep going. I had to keep moving forward, even if I had no idea where I was headed.

I had one goal now—one thing to focus on: getting past the hurt, the betrayal, and the loneliness. I wasn't sure how long it would take or what the road would look like, but I knew one thing for sure. I wasn't going to let them define me. I was going to find my own way out of the darkness.

❦❦❦

8
The Road to Healing

The weeks following my encounter with Naira and the constant reminders of Vraj's betrayal felt like an endless cycle. There were good days, when I managed to put on a semblance of normalcy, but those were few and far between. The rest of the time, I was stuck in my own head, lost in thoughts I didn't want to confront. My body moved through the motions, but my mind lingered in the past.

College was a blur. I attended my lectures, sat through classes, but everything seemed distant. My mind wandered. I didn't feel connected to anyone anymore, even Arjun, who had been my rock throughout this chaos. Arjun could see it too. He noticed the change, and though he never pushed, I could feel his concern.

One afternoon, a few weeks after I'd first confronted Naira, I found myself sitting alone in the canteen. The noise of students laughing, gossiping, and chatting around me felt like an alien sound. It was hard to believe that only a few months ago, I had been right there with them, carefree and happy.

"Bro, you've been distant," Arjun said, sliding into the chair opposite mine. "What's going on with you?"

I sighed and pushed my food aside. I hadn't been hungry for days. "I don't know, Arjun. I'm just... tired of it all. Tired of pretending everything's okay. Tired of seeing them around like nothing happened."

Arjun studied me for a moment, his expression softening. "It's not easy, I know. But Dhruv, you can't let them win. They messed up, sure. But you're letting them control your life now. You need to take control, man. You've got to start living for yourself again."

I looked up at him, his words sinking deep into me. He was right, but it was easier said than done. How could I move on from something that had shattered me so completely? How could I stop myself from feeling this constant ache whenever I saw Vraj or Naira?

I didn't have an answer, but Arjun's unwavering presence reminded me that maybe, just maybe, I could find my way back.

ᐅᐅᐅ

The next few days, I took small steps. I stopped avoiding my friends in college, and instead of retreating into the library or hiding in the corners of the campus, I started sitting with Arjun during breaks. It wasn't easy, but I forced myself to interact. I listened to my classmates talk about their plans for the weekend, their assignments, their dreams. I smiled along with them, pretending like I wasn't broken inside.

But it felt good to be part of the world again, to not be consumed by my own grief.

It wasn't long before Didi noticed the change. One evening, after I had come back from a long day at college, she cornered me in the living room.

"You're doing better, aren't you?" she asked softly, watching me carefully.

I gave her a hesitant smile. "I guess. It's hard to say. But I'm trying."

She nodded, her face full of understanding. "Trying is all that matters. Just don't forget that you're not alone in this. Mumma and Papa don't know the whole story, and I don't plan on telling them anytime soon. But that doesn't mean we can't talk about it, Dhruv. You don't have to keep everything inside."

Her words were comforting, but they also made me feel vulnerable. Didi had always been my protector, my guide, and I knew she was right. I didn't have to shoulder this burden alone. But there was still a part of me that wasn't ready to share the depths of my pain.

ᐅᐅᐅ

That night, as I lay in bed, I thought about everything I had gone through. The heartbreak, the betrayal, the countless moments of doubt and self-blame. I thought about Vraj, about Naira. And I wondered—was there any way to move forward? Was I doomed to be stuck in this cycle forever?

I didn't have an answer. But what I did know was that I couldn't keep looking backward. I couldn't keep punishing myself for something that wasn't my fault. The past had shaped me, yes, but it didn't have to define me.

ᐅᐅᐅ

A week later, I did something I hadn't done in months. I called up Rhea, a friend from college who had been there through a lot of my early days at university. She had always been a cheerful and positive presence in my life, someone who could lighten any room with her laughter. After everything had happened with Vraj and Naira, we had lost touch, but something in me told me that reaching out to her might help.

To my surprise, she picked up on the first ring.

"Hello?" Rhea's voice was warm and familiar, and hearing it made something inside me loosen.

"Hey, Rhea," I said, my voice a little shaky. "It's Dhruv."

There was a pause on the other end, and then, "Dhruv! Oh my god, it's been so long! How are you? How've you been?"

I hesitated before answering. The truth was, I wasn't okay. But I didn't want to burden her with all of it.

"I've been... okay," I said after a moment. "I've just been dealing with some stuff. It's been hard."

She was quiet for a moment, probably sensing the underlying pain in my words. "Do you want to talk about it? I'm here for you, Dhruv."

I smiled faintly, grateful for her kindness. "Maybe another time, Rhea. I'm still trying to figure things out. But I just... I wanted to hear your voice, you know? It's been too long."

She laughed softly. "I understand. But whenever you're ready, just know that I'm here."

We talked for a while longer, and just hearing Rhea's voice, hearing her laugh again, was like a breath of fresh air. It wasn't a solution, but it was a small step toward feeling like myself again.

ᕙᕙᕙ

The road to healing was never going to be easy. Some days were better than others, and there were still moments when the pain would come rushing back, overwhelming me like a wave. But I was learning to cope, learning to live again, even if it was one tiny moment at a time.

And that was enough.

As the days stretched into weeks, I slowly began to rebuild parts of my life that I thought I had lost forever. It was like taking small steps on a path that seemed never-ending, but with every little milestone, I felt stronger. The pain was still there, lingering in the background, but it wasn't as all-consuming as it used to be. I was learning to live with it, rather than letting it dictate my every move.

ppp

It was a Sunday morning when I first felt the urge to step outside of my comfort zone completely. I had been cooped up in my room for days, only coming out when absolutely necessary—mostly to attend college or grab a bite to eat. But that day, I knew I had to do something different. I couldn't let this chapter of my life define me forever.

I decided to go for a walk around Marine Drive. The cool breeze, the endless stretch of the sea—it had always been my sanctuary. The place where I could clear my head and just be.

I wore a simple T-shirt and jeans, nothing special, but it felt good to be out of the house. To breathe in the fresh air and let the sea's rhythm calm my mind. As I walked along the promenade, my thoughts drifted back to the days when everything had felt perfect. When I had been so hopeful about the future, with Naira and Vraj by my side, and everything seemed right in the world. But now, that seemed like a distant memory, one I could hardly reach.

ppp

"Dhruv!" A voice interrupted my thoughts, pulling me out of my head.

I turned around and saw Arjun jogging up to me. His face lit up when he saw me, and for a moment, it felt like the world was just a little bit brighter.

"What are you doing here?" I asked, raising an eyebrow as he caught up to me.

Arjun grinned. "Same as you, I guess. Just trying to clear my head. Can I walk with you?"

I nodded, glad for the company. The walk felt easier with him by my side, as we talked about random things—college, movies, anything other than what was really weighing on my mind. For a while, it was like I wasn't carrying the world on my shoulders. It was a relief, a small but significant break from the emotional turmoil I had been living in.

We walked along the coastline for hours, and for the first time in a long time, I felt something like peace settle within me. I didn't have all the answers yet, and the wounds weren't fully healed, but I was starting to see that there was more to life than the pain I had been stuck in.

ᗡᗡᗡ

When I got home that evening, Mumma noticed the change immediately. She gave me a knowing smile as I entered the living room.

"Out for a walk, I see," she said casually, glancing up from the book she was reading.

I nodded. "Yeah. Just needed to get some fresh air."

She studied me carefully for a moment, then set her book down. "Dhruv, I know you're still hurting, and I can see that you're trying. But you don't have to carry all of this alone. Your papa and I—we're here for you, always."

I smiled faintly, feeling a surge of gratitude for her. "Thanks, Mumma. I'm trying. I really am."

She gave me a soft hug, her arms comforting, and for a moment, it felt like everything would be okay.

ᐅᐅᐅ

Days turned into weeks, and life slowly started to take on a different rhythm. I was still a long way from completely letting go, but I had begun to rebuild my sense of self. College felt less suffocating. The sight of Vraj didn't send me into a spiral of anger and hurt every time anymore. I had learned to accept that he would be there, and while I could never look at him the same way again, I could still coexist with him. For my peace of mind, I had to find a way to exist in the same space without it consuming me.

Naira, on the other hand, was still a complicated issue. I didn't know what to feel when I saw her in class or when I passed her in the hallway. It was hard to forget the betrayal, but there were times when I could almost forget the pain—almost forgive her, but not quite. The healing process was so much slower when it came to her.

☙☙☙

One evening, about a month after that walk along Marine Drive, I decided to visit the same spot again. This time, it was just me and the city, the sound of the waves crashing against the shore, the distant hum of cars, and the light breeze that carried with it the scent of the ocean.

I was standing there, lost in my thoughts when I received a message from Rhea. She had texted me a few times after our conversation, checking in, and today, she asked, "How are you holding up, Dhruv? Any better?"

I smiled at the screen, grateful for her friendship. "I'm getting there. Slowly but surely."

Rhea's reply was immediate: "That's good to hear. I know it's tough, but don't rush it. Take your time. I'm here whenever you need to talk."

I leaned against the railing, looking out at the vastness of the sea. I wasn't ready to forget. I didn't think I would ever forget. But I was starting to heal, piece by piece, day by day.

☙☙☙

A few more weeks went by, and life seemed to settle into a new normal. I was managing better, focusing more on my studies, spending time with friends who genuinely cared for me, and, most importantly, I was beginning to focus on myself.

I had stopped avoiding things that reminded me of my pain. I started reconnecting with old friends, and even began pursuing some hobbies I had long abandoned—photography, reading, and playing the guitar. It wasn't about trying to distract myself. It was about rediscovering pieces of me that had gotten lost in the chaos.

ᐅᐅᐅ

But as I walked through the campus one afternoon, I saw Vraj sitting with his friends near the fountain. I hadn't planned on confronting him, but there was something about the sight of him laughing with his friends that triggered something deep within me. That old feeling of anger and betrayal flared up again, but this time, I wasn't crushed by it.

I walked up to him, my footsteps purposeful. His eyes met mine, and for a moment, it felt like the whole world stopped. He looked different—still the same Vraj, but there was something in his gaze, something unreadable. He didn't say anything right away, but I could see the unease in his eyes.

"Dhruv," he said softly, his voice low. "I never meant for things to turn out like this."

I looked at him for a long moment before responding. "You should have thought about that before you hurt me, Vraj."

His face tightened with regret, but I wasn't angry anymore. I wasn't looking for an apology. I didn't need one from him. I had already moved on in my own way.

"I don't expect forgiveness, Dhruv," he said quietly. "But I'm sorry."

I nodded, feeling a sense of finality wash over me. "I know."

I turned and walked away, not looking back.

And for the first time in a long time, I felt lighter.

ᗞᗞᗞ

9
The Path Forward

The weeks after that encounter with Vraj were a blur, but in a good way. I had started to feel more like myself again. It was as though the heavy weight I'd been carrying around for months had finally begun to lift. Sure, the memories of the past still lingered, like shadows that couldn't quite be shaken off, but they no longer controlled my life.

I still felt occasional pangs of anger or sadness when I thought about what happened with Naira and Vraj, but now, those feelings were more like distant echoes. It wasn't perfect, but it was progress. And for once, I wasn't focusing on the past or trying to figure out what went wrong. I was learning to live again.

ᏯᏯᏯ

One evening, as I was sitting in the living room, scrolling through some old photos on my phone, Didi came in and sat down beside me. She had noticed how much better I seemed lately, but she never asked about it directly. I guess she knew I wasn't ready to talk yet, but I could tell she was still keeping an eye on me, as older siblings often do.

"You know, I've been thinking," Didi said, breaking the silence. "You've been doing so much better lately. I'm proud of you, Dhruv. I really am."

I looked at her and smiled. "Thanks, Didi. It means a lot to me."

She tilted her head and smiled back. "You've grown a lot through all this. I can see it. You've come a long way from that broken person you were a couple of months ago."

I nodded, a faint smile tugging at my lips. "It hasn't been easy, but... I'm getting there. It's still a process, but I'm trying."

"You know," she continued, "I think it's time you start doing something for yourself. Something that makes you happy. You've been so focused on everyone else, trying to fix everything, but what about you? You need to take care of yourself, too."

Her words hit me harder than I expected. I had been so wrapped up in the fallout of everything that I hadn't really stopped to think about my own happiness.

"What do you mean?" I asked, genuinely curious.

Didi shrugged, a mischievous glint in her eyes. "I don't know. Maybe join that photography club you've been talking about.

Or finally start that book you've been meaning to write. Whatever it is, just do something for you. You deserve it."

Her encouragement was exactly what I needed. I had been avoiding my own desires, putting my own needs last, but now, I could see that it was time to take a step forward. To focus on my passions, the things that used to make me feel alive before everything fell apart.

ᘔᘔᘔ

The next day, I finally made a decision. I took out my camera—the one that had been sitting in the corner of my room, collecting dust for months—and dusted it off. I hadn't picked it up since before everything happened with Naira and Vraj. The thought of photography used to fill me with excitement, but somewhere along the way, it had become a painful reminder of everything I had lost.

But today was different.

I walked out of the house, ready to explore the world around me through the lens of my camera. I didn't have a particular destination in mind, but I felt the need to capture the beauty of the world, even if it was just through the streets of Mumbai, the city that had always been my home.

As I walked through the crowded streets, the bustling markets, and the quieter lanes, I saw things I hadn't noticed before. The way the sunlight filtered through the trees in the park, the colors of the street art on the walls, the smiles of strangers passing by. The world, despite everything, was still full of beauty.

I clicked away, each shot capturing a fleeting moment, and in that moment, I realized something—I was beginning to heal. Slowly, but surely, I was finding pieces of myself again.

ᑭᑭᑭ

That evening, I found myself in the same spot by Marine Drive, watching the sun set over the horizon. The colors of the sky reflected in the water, painting everything in hues of orange and purple. It was beautiful. Peaceful.

I took a deep breath, feeling the cool breeze against my skin. The city had always been my refuge, my constant in the ever-changing chaos of life. And now, I was starting to feel at home in it again, even with the scars of the past still fresh in my heart.

My phone buzzed in my pocket. I pulled it out and saw a message from Rhea.

"How's your day been?"

I smiled and typed back, "It's been good. I took some photos, just got out of my head for a bit. Feeling better."

"That's awesome, Dhruv! I knew you could do it. You're stronger than you think."

I stared at her message for a moment, the words sinking in. She was right. I was stronger than I had given myself credit for. I wasn't the same person I had been when all of this started, but maybe that wasn't such a bad thing.

I sat there for a while, just watching the waves roll in. The sounds of the city, the voices of people laughing, the honking of horns, all faded away as I focused on the present. The past had shaped me, but it didn't define me.

ᐅᐅᐅ

A few days later, I decided to take Didi's advice seriously. I joined a photography club on campus. It wasn't a huge step, but it felt like the right one. I wanted to surround myself with like-minded people, to share something I loved, and perhaps, learn to enjoy it again without the weight of the past holding me back.

As I entered the first meeting, I felt a mixture of nervousness and excitement. The club members were welcoming, and we spent the next few hours discussing our favorite styles of photography, sharing tips, and planning upcoming photo walks. For the first time in a long while, I felt a sense of purpose.

ᐅᐅᐅ

Life, as it always does, began to fall back into a routine. I spent time with Arjun, slowly opening up to him more about what I had been through. I began to reconnect with old friends, and though I still struggled with the memory of Vraj and Naira, I knew that the road to healing wasn't a straight line. Some days would be harder than others, but the important thing was that I was moving forward.

There were still nights when I would lie awake, memories of the past flooding my mind. But each time, I reminded myself that the present was what I had to focus on. The future was still uncertain, but it was mine to shape.

And in that moment, as I sat by the sea, with the sound of the waves crashing against the shore, I realized that I was no longer the boy who had been broken by betrayal. I was Dhruv—the boy who had survived, who had grown, and who was ready to embrace whatever the future held.

It wasn't going to be easy, but for the first time in a long time, I was ready for whatever came next.

ppp

As time went on, I found myself getting lost in my new routines—small moments that felt significant because they were my own. Each day seemed a little less heavy, and with each passing week, I grew more confident in my ability to handle life without letting the past hold me back.

The photography club turned out to be a perfect outlet. I learned more about the art than I had expected, from the technical aspects of lighting to capturing moments in ways I'd never considered. I spent weekends exploring different parts of the city with my camera, trying to capture the soul of Mumbai through my lens. Each picture told a story—whether it was a candid shot of a street vendor or a peaceful morning at the beach. I was seeing the world through a new perspective, a fresh set of eyes.

ppp

It wasn't just photography that was slowly reawakening a part of me I thought I had lost forever. I was beginning to reconnect with myself in a way that felt right. Little by little, I started to remember who I was before everything happened. Before the heartbreak. Before the betrayal.

But the road to true healing was far from over.

ppp

One afternoon, as I was waiting for my photography club meeting to start, I ran into Anaya—Naira. We hadn't spoken much after the fallout. She had been staying distant, and so had I. I wasn't sure what to feel when I saw her, but I couldn't ignore the fact that there was something unresolved between us.

I had spent so many sleepless nights wondering what I should say if I ever ran into her again. I hadn't forgiven her, not fully, but I also realized I wasn't going to find peace by keeping her at arm's length forever.

I had always thought of Naira as my closest friend. And that didn't change overnight.

"Dhruv," she said, her voice soft. "Hey."

I looked up, taken aback by how much she had changed in the few months since we last spoke. There was a sadness in her eyes, but also something else—a hint of guilt, maybe.

I stood up slowly, uncertain. "Naira."

There was an awkward silence for a few moments, neither of us knowing what to say. She glanced down at the ground, fidgeting with her hands.

"I... I've been meaning to talk to you," she said hesitantly.

I raised an eyebrow. "About what?"

She hesitated, then spoke again, quieter this time. "I don't expect you to forgive me. I know I've hurt you in ways that can never be undone, but I want you to know I regret everything. The way things went down between us... I never wanted to hurt you, Dhruv."

The words hit me harder than I thought they would. I felt a flood of emotion—anger, sadness, confusion—but there was also something else. A part of me that still cared for her. A part of me that missed the friendship we had shared before all of this had happened.

I crossed my arms, leaning against the wall as I processed her words. "I don't know what you expect from me, Naira. I don't even know if I want to talk about this anymore."

She took a step forward, her voice shaky. "I just... I just want you to know that I'm sorry. I don't expect forgiveness, but I'm sorry for how I treated you. For everything."

For a moment, I stood there in silence, staring at her, as if waiting for the right words to come to me. But there was nothing. I couldn't bring myself to say anything back—not yet.

"Look, I don't know where to go from here," I said finally. "But I'm not that person I was before. I can't pretend like it didn't happen."

She nodded, her eyes wet with tears. "I understand. I just... I wanted to tell you I'm sorry, and that I hope, one day, you can find it in your heart to forgive me."

I couldn't look her in the eye anymore, so I turned and began walking away, leaving her standing there. I didn't know if I'd ever forgive her. Maybe I would, but not yet. Not when the wounds were still fresh.

But it didn't matter. What mattered was that I was finally facing the past. I was no longer running away from it.

ᐅᐅᐅ

Later that week, I decided to visit the café I used to frequent with Naira and Vraj before everything changed. I wasn't sure why I went back there. Maybe it was just because the place felt like a part of my old life. The place where I used to laugh, talk about silly things, and forget the world around me.

I ordered a cappuccino and sat at the same corner table by the window, looking out at the busy street. The café was still the same—cozy, with dim lighting and the aroma of fresh coffee wafting through the air. But it felt different now. The memories associated with it were tainted, clouded with the pain of the past.

But I was learning to accept that it was okay to have those memories. They were a part of me, whether I liked it or not.

ƿƿƿ

The more I focused on moving forward, the more I realized how important it was to surround myself with the right people. My college friends, Arjun, and Rhea had been my pillars of support throughout this journey. But I knew I couldn't keep hiding behind their kindness forever. I had to start taking ownership of my own happiness again.

One afternoon, I sat down with Rhea after class. We grabbed coffee at a small café nearby, and as we sat down at a table, I found myself opening up to her in a way I hadn't done with anyone else in a long time.

"Rhea, I've been thinking a lot about everything," I began. "About Naira, Vraj... everything that happened. I realized that I've spent so much time letting the past dictate who I am. It's like I've been holding onto the pain, thinking it would somehow fix things."

She nodded, her expression soft. "You're allowed to feel what you're feeling, Dhruv. But you also have to realize that it's okay to let go. Holding onto that pain doesn't serve you—it only holds you back."

I took a deep breath, feeling the weight of her words. "I know. But it's not easy. There are days when I feel like I'm drowning in it. And then there are days when I feel like I'm making progress, but it's still hard to shake off the memories."

"You will," she said gently. "It's a process. Just keep taking it one step at a time. You don't have to do it all at once. Just trust that you'll get there."

Her encouragement gave me the strength I needed to keep pushing forward. Slowly, I began to understand that moving on didn't mean forgetting. It didn't mean erasing the past from my mind. It simply meant accepting that I couldn't change what happened, but I could still shape my future.

ᐅᐅᐅ

The next few months were a mix of ups and downs. I started to get more involved in the photography club, and I even started submitting some of my work to local exhibitions. I was building my confidence, piece by piece, and learning to trust myself again. I spent more time with Arjun, Rhea, and my other friends, and each day felt a little more balanced.

The pain of betrayal wasn't gone, but it wasn't controlling me anymore. I was learning to live alongside it, to let it shape me into someone stronger, someone who was no longer afraid to move forward.

One evening, as I was looking through some of my photos at home, I realized something important: the hardest part of healing wasn't about forgetting what happened. It was about forgiving myself for allowing it to hurt me for so long.

It was a process, and it wasn't easy. But it was mine to take.

And in that moment, as I looked out at the Mumbai skyline, I felt a glimmer of hope—a belief that maybe, just maybe, the best was yet to come.

ᐅᐅᐅ

10
The Final Step

It had been a few months since I had started feeling like I was finally regaining control over my life. Each day was a little easier than the one before, though the scars of betrayal would always be a part of me. The more I focused on my passions, like photography, and the more I reconnected with friends like Arjun and Rhea, the further away the pain seemed. Still, there were days when the memories of Naira and Vraj would creep back into my mind like unwelcome shadows. But this time, I didn't let them take me under.

"Healing doesn't mean the damage never existed. It means the damage no longer controls our lives."

That quote, which I had read in an old book, stayed with me. It resonated deeply with me, because the truth was—though I could never fully erase what had happened, I had finally taken control of how it would affect me going forward. I was no longer that heartbroken, lost kid who had given up on everything.

One evening, as I was working on a project for the photography club, I received a message from Didi. She asked me if I wanted to go out for dinner with her and Mumma and Papa. It had been a while since we did anything together, just the four of us. With everything that had happened, I had grown distant, though not intentionally. I hadn't realized how much I missed those small, simple family moments.

I texted back, **"Sure. It's been a while. I'd love to."**

That evening, we went to our favorite little family restaurant. Mumma and Papa were still as lively as ever, cracking jokes and reminiscing about old times. Didi was teasing me about my photography obsession, saying I was turning into a "professional snapper," and Mumma just smiled at me, her eyes warm with pride.

As we sat at the table, I realized something I hadn't thought about in a long time. **"Family is the only thing that remains when everything else falls apart."** That simple thought had an immense weight. No matter what happened with Naira or Vraj, no matter the heartbreak or the betrayal, my family had always been there for me.

It was these moments—moments with my family, with people who genuinely cared for me—that helped me piece myself back together.

ﬧﬧﬧ

The following days continued on in a similar rhythm. I threw myself into my work for the photography club. I attended classes. I spent time with my friends. And in between it all, I took moments to reflect on how far I had come.

Yet, the day was coming that I had been dreading and, at the same time, anticipating.

The semester was nearing its end, and I had just finished a big project for my photography class. It was something I had worked on for weeks, capturing different aspects of the city, of life itself. I had put my heart into it.

The exhibition was scheduled for the weekend, and I was feeling a mix of nervousness and excitement. It wasn't just about showing my work—it was about standing before everyone and saying, **"I've moved on. This is who I am now."**

▷▷▷

The day of the exhibition arrived. The gallery was small, but it was full of energy. People were admiring the pieces on the walls, and my heart raced as I stood in front of my collection. This was my first real chance to show the world what I was capable of—not just in photography, but in life itself.

As I walked around the room, I heard people complimenting my photos, and for the first time in a long while, I felt proud of something I had done for myself. It wasn't for anyone else. It wasn't about impressing Naira or Vraj. It was my work, my expression.

And then, as if fate had planned it, I saw her. Naira. She was standing near the entrance, looking at a photo of the Mumbai skyline. I froze for a moment, unsure of how to approach her—or if I even should.

"The past is never truly gone. But it no longer controls you."

That thought crossed my mind as I took a deep breath and walked towards her. I wasn't going to avoid the confrontation anymore. Not this time. I had faced my demons, and I wasn't going to shy away from this moment.

Naira turned around when she heard my footsteps. She looked at me, her face showing a mix of surprise and hesitation.

"Dhruv," she said quietly, her voice almost apologetic. "I... I didn't know you were part of this exhibition."

I smiled faintly. "Yeah, I've been working on it for a while."

There was a brief, awkward silence between us. I couldn't help but notice the guilt in her eyes, the same guilt that had been there the last time we spoke. But now, I wasn't angry. I had long ago realized that holding onto that anger would only continue to hurt me.

"I'm sorry, Dhruv," she said, her voice cracking slightly. "I know I can't undo what I did. I... I don't expect you to forgive me. But I am truly sorry for everything."

I nodded, the words slipping easily from my mouth now, words I had been holding inside for months. "I know, Naira. I know. And I've forgiven you. Not for your sake, but for mine. I've let go of the anger. I don't have any room for it anymore."

There was a look of relief on her face. "I'm glad to hear that." She paused, looking at the photos around us. "These are really good, Dhruv. I always knew you had a talent for this."

"Thanks," I replied, genuinely appreciative of the compliment. "I've been putting in a lot of work. It's been helping me focus on the present, you know?"

We stood in silence for a while, not knowing where to take the conversation next. But then, something unexpected happened.

Naira reached out and placed a hand on my arm. "I... I hope you're okay, Dhruv. Truly."

I looked down at her hand, then back into her eyes. "I am. I really am. It took time, but I'm better now."

She smiled, her expression softening. "I'm glad."

I didn't say anything more. I didn't need to. We had said everything that needed to be said. The past couldn't be changed, but we could both move forward with peace in our hearts. And that's what mattered.

ϡϡϡ

As I stood there, watching Naira walk away, I realized something profound. **"Sometimes, the hardest part of healing is not the pain we carry, but the forgiveness we need to give ourselves."** I had forgiven her, yes, but more importantly, I had forgiven myself. I had stopped blaming myself for the mistakes we both made.

I walked away from the gallery that evening with my head held high, not because I had solved everything, but because I had learned to let go. The chapter with Naira and Vraj had closed, but I was ready to start a new one. Not for them, not for anyone else—but for me.

I was finally free.

As the days passed after the exhibition, I found myself feeling a sense of calm that I hadn't felt in a long time. The weight of the past—of Naira, of Vraj—had finally started to feel lighter. It wasn't that I had forgotten everything, but I had come to terms with it. I was no longer consumed by anger, resentment, or the endless cycle of "what ifs." Instead, I started to live in the present, focusing on what was in front of me rather than dwelling on what was behind.

I spent more time with my friends, Arjun and Rhea, as they had always been there to help me navigate through the storm. Arjun, with his carefree attitude and wit, had a way of making even the darkest days feel a little brighter. Rhea, on the other hand, was my anchor. Her unwavering support and understanding had kept me grounded when I felt like I was drowning in my emotions.

One evening, as I was hanging out with Arjun, we ended up in a deep conversation about everything that had happened. We were sitting on the roof of the college building, watching the city lights twinkle beneath us, and I found myself talking more openly than I had before.

"You know, Arjun, I still don't understand how things went so wrong," I said, my voice heavy with the remnants of old pain. "I trusted them both. And I thought we were all on the same page, you know? But they both let me down."

Arjun took a deep breath, his gaze fixed on the horizon. "It's not easy, man. Trust is one of the hardest things to rebuild, especially after it's broken like that. But what you have to remember is that it's not your fault. People make choices. And sometimes, those choices hurt, but it's not on you to carry their burden."

I nodded slowly, taking in his words. "I know, but it still stings. Every time I think about it, it's like a punch to the gut. Like I wasn't enough, you know?"

He chuckled softly, nudging me with his elbow. "Dhruv, listen to me. You are more than enough. No one should ever make you feel like you're less than that. You're a good person. You've got a big heart. Don't ever forget that."

The sincerity in his voice made something inside me shift. I had spent so much time questioning my worth, blaming myself for what happened, but maybe it was time to stop. Maybe it was time to start believing in the version of myself that didn't need validation from anyone else.

I had my own worth, and no one could take that away from me.

☙☙☙

As the semester came to an end, I began to notice the change in myself. I wasn't the same person who had walked into college months ago, broken and unsure. I was growing stronger, more confident, and more aware of my own boundaries. My photography had become not just a hobby, but a passion—a way of expressing myself in ways I never thought possible. Each click of the camera felt like a step forward, a step away from the past.

And then, one evening, as I was sitting in the park, my phone buzzed. It was a message from Mumma: **"Come home early tonight. We need to talk."**

A wave of anxiety hit me. I knew Mumma and Papa had been worried about me ever since they found out what had happened with Naira and Vraj. They hadn't pressured me to talk about it, but I knew they were always concerned about how deeply it had affected me. I hadn't discussed the whole situation with them in detail, and part of me had been avoiding that conversation.

But maybe it was time. Maybe it was time to open up to them.

☙☙☙

When I got home that evening, I was greeted by Mumma's warm smile, but there was a hint of concern in her eyes. Didi was sitting next to her, her face thoughtful.

"Dhruv," Mumma said softly, "we need to talk about everything that happened. We know it's been hard for you, and we've seen the way you've been carrying this weight. We just want you to know that we're here for you, no matter what."

I sat down across from them, feeling a lump in my throat. I had never really talked about the depth of my pain with Mumma and Papa. I had kept my feelings to myself, not wanting to burden them with my heartache.

But Mumma reached out, placing her hand gently over mine. "You don't have to carry it alone, beta. We know it's been difficult. But remember, we are your family. And we will always stand by you, no matter what."

I could feel the tears welling up in my eyes, but I held them back. **"I've been trying to deal with everything on my own,"** I said, my voice thick with emotion. **"I didn't want to disappoint you. But I've been feeling like I'm drowning, Mumma. Every day it's like I'm carrying a weight I can't shake off. I thought maybe time would heal it, but it hasn't. And sometimes, I feel like I'm not even the same person anymore."**

Didi looked at me with understanding, her voice gentle. "Dhruv, you're still the same person. You've just been through something really painful, and that changes you. But it doesn't erase who you are. You're strong. And you're allowed to feel all of this. It's okay to hurt, but don't let it define you."

Mumma squeezed my hand. "We're proud of you, beta. You're growing. You're healing. And that's what matters. Just take it one day at a time. We're here to help, always."

ᗰᗰᗰ

For the first time in months, I felt a sense of peace. It was like a burden had been lifted off my chest. I didn't have to pretend to be fine anymore. I didn't have to carry the weight of my emotions alone. Mumma, Papa, and Didi were right. **"Healing is not linear, and it's okay to have bad days. But it's important to keep moving forward, even if it's just one step at a time."**

ᗰᗰᗰ

A few weeks later, as the summer break began, I found myself standing at the beach, camera in hand. The sun was setting, casting a warm, golden glow across the horizon. The waves crashed gently against the shore, the sound soothing in its rhythm. I clicked a few shots, capturing the beauty of the moment.

It was in that moment, standing there with the wind in my hair and the sound of the ocean filling my ears, that I realized how far I had come. I wasn't the same person I had been when I first arrived in Mumbai. The pain of betrayal was still there, but it didn't control me anymore. I had learned to live with it, to move past it, to make peace with it.

And in that moment, I found a sense of freedom. **"The past may have shaped me, but it no longer defines me. I define who I am, and I'm ready to move forward."**

I had finally found my peace.

11
Finding Peace

It had been a few months since that day at the beach. The storm inside me had settled, and now, I was in a place where I could finally breathe again. Things weren't perfect—life never really is—but they were better. It was as if the pieces of me that had been shattered over the past year had slowly started to come together, bit by bit.

I had taken up more freelance work in photography. Some of my projects were small—capturing portraits for local businesses or working on event shoots—but they gave me a sense of purpose, a chance to express myself in ways words could never capture. Each click of the camera felt like a release, a way of letting go of the things I couldn't say.

I spent more time with my friends too. Arjun and Rhea had been the pillars I didn't even realize I needed. They weren't just friends; they were family. Arjun, with his loud jokes and constant energy, kept me laughing even when I didn't feel like it. Rhea, who had always been so patient with me, was there to listen whenever I needed to talk.

The more I opened up to them, the more I realized how important it was to surround myself with people who cared for me. **"Surround yourself with those who lift you higher,"** was a phrase I had come across a few weeks ago, and it felt truer than ever.

$$\triangleright\triangleright\triangleright$$

One evening, I was sitting at a café with Rhea, sipping on a hot cup of chai. The city outside was buzzing with life, the traffic creating a constant hum in the background. But inside, it was quiet—just the two of us, chatting about everything and nothing.

"So, Dhruv," Rhea said, raising an eyebrow. "Have you thought about what you're doing next year after this semester ends? You know, for your photography? It feels like you've really found your rhythm with it."

I smiled, a little unsure but also hopeful. "Honestly, Rhea, I'm not entirely sure. But for the first time in a while, I'm actually excited about the future. I think I want to focus more on my photography, see where it takes me. It feels right."

She grinned, her eyes sparkling. "That's great, Dhruv. You've worked so hard for this. Whatever you decide to do, I know you'll make it happen."

Her belief in me, her unwavering support, was a reminder of how far I had come. **"The people who are meant for you will never let you go. No matter how tough things get."**

ᚦᚦᚦ

As I was thinking about my future, I realized that the pain of the past no longer had a hold on me. The flashbacks of betrayal, the days I spent crying into my pillow, they were still there in the back of my mind, but they no longer controlled my every thought. **"Time doesn't heal all wounds, but it does teach us how to live with them."**

That thought echoed in my mind as I walked down the street one afternoon, heading to a photography shoot. I had come to understand that healing wasn't a destination—it was a journey. Sometimes, it felt like I was taking two steps forward and one step back. But that was okay. Progress was progress, no matter how small.

I had learned to forgive. Not just Naira and Vraj, but also myself. I had learned to forgive myself for allowing myself to be hurt, for putting my heart on the line and trusting the wrong people. But now, I knew better. **"Forgiveness is not for the other person, it's for you."**

ᚦᚦᚦ

One evening, after I had finished a photography gig, I found myself at the same spot in the park where I had sat months ago, alone with my thoughts. The sky was painted in shades of purple and pink as the sun set, and I took a deep breath, feeling the cool evening air fill my lungs. There was something calming about this place, something grounding.

I pulled out my phone and began scrolling through my photos from the past few months. I hadn't shared most of them with anyone. They were just for me, a personal journey that I wasn't ready to show the world yet. But looking at them now, I realized something. Each photo captured not just an image, but a feeling. A moment. A story.

"Art is not what you see, but what you make others see." That quote, by Edgar Degas, came to mind as I looked through the pictures. Each shot I took, each moment I captured, told the story of my healing. Every frame was a reflection of my growth, my struggles, my pain—and finally, my peace.

ᗑᗑᗑ

As I sat there, deep in thought, I received a message from Mumma: **"Dinner at home tonight? Papa is making your favorite dal fry."**

I smiled, my heart swelling with warmth. My family. They had always been my constant, my safe haven in the midst of chaos. No matter what happened outside, no matter what heartbreak I faced, I could always count on them.

When I got home that evening, Mumma and Papa were already seated at the dining table, and Didi was joking with them about something. The smell of the dal fry filled the house, and for a moment, everything felt normal again. Peaceful.

I sat down at the table, taking a bite of the dal fry, and then I looked at each of them—Mumma, Papa, and Didi—and I realized how lucky I was to have them in my life.

"Family is not an important thing, it's everything." That was something I had come to understand with every passing day.

ppp

It was a simple evening, one of those that felt perfect in its simplicity. And yet, it was in these moments that I found my peace. I wasn't the same person I had been when I first arrived in Mumbai, and I wasn't the person I had been months ago, drowning in heartbreak. I had learned to let go, to heal, to forgive—and most importantly, to love myself again.

In that moment, surrounded by the warmth of my family and the love of my friends, I understood one undeniable truth: **"Sometimes, the greatest form of strength is in knowing when to let go."**

And as I sat there, enjoying the meal, I realized that the person I had always been waiting for—the person who could save me—was never someone outside of myself. I had saved myself. I had built myself back up from the pieces of my broken heart, and now I was finally whole again.

ppp

The journey wasn't over yet. There would always be days when the past tried to creep back into my life, when the pain of betrayal would resurface. But I knew now that I was stronger than it. **"What doesn't kill you, makes you stronger."** I had proved that to myself.

The road ahead wasn't clear, but it was mine to walk. And I was ready. **"The best way to predict your future is to create it."** And that's exactly what I was doing, one step at a time.

ᠹᠹᠹ

The days continued to move by, flowing like the calm waves of the ocean I'd once stood by. The more time passed, the more I realized that healing wasn't an event—it was a process. **"Healing is not linear. Some days, you'll feel like you're moving forward, and on others, you'll feel like you're stuck. But that's okay,"** I reminded myself often. And with each passing day, I could feel myself becoming more at peace with the choices I had made and the person I was becoming.

Rhea, as always, was my sounding board. We talked about everything—our classes, our experiences, our future plans. It felt like with her around, there was always an opportunity for laughter, even on the toughest of days. That day, she was particularly excited about something.

"So, Dhruv, have you thought about applying for the photography internship at that art gallery? It could be an amazing opportunity for you," she asked, her eyes wide with enthusiasm.

I blinked, taken aback by her suggestion. I had always focused on small gigs and freelance work, but an internship at an art gallery? That sounded like a dream. "I don't know, Rhea," I replied hesitantly. "I've never thought of it that seriously, you know? I've been too caught up in the aftermath of everything that happened."

She leaned in, her voice serious. "Dhruv, you have the talent. You've grown so much in the past few months. I've seen it. You can't keep doubting yourself. Take the leap. I'm sure you'll get it. Just apply."

Her words, filled with belief and encouragement, felt like a spark of motivation that I hadn't realized I needed. It made me realize how much I had been holding myself back—not just because of the betrayal, but because of the fear that had crept in after it. Fear that I wasn't good enough, that I wasn't worthy of success or happiness. "The only limits that exist are the ones you place on yourself." Rhea had pushed me to see beyond my self-imposed barriers, and for the first time in a long while, I felt ready to move forward.

That evening, I sat down in front of my laptop and searched for the internship details. My heart pounded in my chest as I read the requirements, the duties, and the skills they were looking for. I knew I wasn't perfect. I knew I still had a long way to go, but I also knew that this was an opportunity I couldn't pass up. With a deep breath, I clicked on the 'Apply' button.

ᑭᑭᑭ

A few weeks later, I received an email confirming that I had been selected for an interview. My heart raced as I read the words. This was it. A real step forward. I told Rhea immediately, and her excitement mirrored mine.

"You did it!" she exclaimed. "I knew you could. Now, go and crush that interview. Show them what Dhruv is made of!"

The day of the interview came, and I felt a mix of nerves and excitement. I had prepared as much as I could—practiced my answers, researched the gallery, and chosen a few of my best photographs to showcase. As I walked into the gallery for the interview, I was greeted by the warm, welcoming staff. The atmosphere inside was calming—white walls lined with stunning art pieces, each telling its own story.

I walked into the interview room, where a woman in her mid-thirties sat behind a desk. She looked up from her papers and smiled warmly. "Dhruv, it's great to meet you. I've heard so much about your work."

The words were like music to my ears. All the months of self-doubt, all the pain, seemed to melt away in that moment.

I sat down and began talking about my passion for photography, my experiences, and my vision for the future. I wasn't nervous anymore. I spoke with confidence and conviction. This was my moment, and I wasn't going to let it slip away.

By the end of the interview, I could tell that it had gone well. The woman gave me a nod of approval. "We'll be in touch soon. Thank you for your time, Dhruv."

I walked out of the gallery feeling like I was on top of the world. The storm inside me had finally calmed, and I had stepped into the next chapter of my life with confidence and purpose.

ppp

When the acceptance email came in a week later, I couldn't believe it. **"Congratulations, Dhruv. You've been selected for the photography internship at our gallery. We're excited to have you on board."**

I was over the moon. It wasn't just about the internship—it was about proving to myself that I was capable of more. That I was worthy of more.

That night, I celebrated with my family. Mumma and Papa were so proud of me, their smiles shining brighter than any success I could achieve. Didi was teasing me, calling me the next big thing in photography.

"I always knew you had it in you, Dhruv," Mumma said, her voice filled with emotion. "We're so proud of you."

Papa hugged me, his big hands strong and comforting. "This is just the beginning. You've made us proud, beta."

It was in moments like these that I realized what truly mattered. Not the success, not the recognition, but the love and support of those who cared for me. It was their belief in me that gave me the strength to keep moving forward.

⌖⌖⌖

Weeks passed, and the internship began. It was everything I had hoped for and more. I found myself immersed in a world of art, learning from professionals, and growing in ways I never thought possible. Every task, from photographing the exhibits to helping organize events, felt like an opportunity to learn and expand my skills. And through it all, I couldn't help but feel grateful.

There were moments, of course, when the shadows of the past crept in. There were days when I'd walk into a coffee shop and see a couple laughing together, and for a split second, I'd think about Naira and Vraj. But then, I'd remember how far I had come. **"The past is a place of reference, not a place of residence."** I had learned to let go, and while I would never forget the pain, I knew that I had the power to choose how it defined me.

⌖⌖⌖

One evening, after a long day at the gallery, I was walking home when I received a call from Arjun.

"Hey, man! I was thinking, how about we catch up tonight? It's been a while since we hung out."

I smiled to myself. It felt good to know that I had people like Arjun, who always knew when I needed a little distraction.

We met up at our usual spot—our favorite late-night food joint, where we always laughed about life, talked about our dreams, and shared random stories.

"So, how's life treating you, Dhruv? You're looking way happier lately," Arjun said, taking a sip of his drink.

I smiled, my heart light. **"I'm good, Arjun. Better than I've ever been, honestly."**

He gave me a knowing look. "It's that photography, isn't it? You've found your peace in it."

I nodded. **"Yeah. I think I've finally figured out that happiness doesn't come from anyone else. It comes from within. And right now, I'm just focused on doing what I love and letting the rest fall into place."**

Arjun raised his glass. "Cheers to that, my friend. You've come a long way. I'm proud of you."

פפפ

And in that moment, I realized that everything I had gone through—the pain, the betrayal, the heartache—had led me here. To this place. To this peace.

"The struggles you face today are the strength you feel tomorrow." And I had never felt stronger.

The journey wasn't over yet, but I was ready for whatever came next.

12
The Quiet Strength of Moving On

Months had passed since that fateful day when I had learned of the betrayal. Since then, I had rebuilt my life in ways I never thought possible. Yet, despite all the progress I'd made, there were still days when the past would rise up like a shadow, silently reminding me of what I had lost. **"The past is never where you think you left it,"** and sometimes, it would catch me off guard. But what I had come to realize was that these moments weren't signs of weakness; they were signs of growth.

I had started to see the beauty in those quiet moments, the ones where the world wasn't moving at a frenetic pace. I spent weekends at the park, walking aimlessly, just letting my thoughts flow. It was in these moments that I truly understood what it meant to heal. Healing wasn't about erasing the past; it was about making peace with it. **"Time heals nothing, but it gives you the ability to deal with what's left."**

I'd found solace in the simplest things—watching the clouds drift by, listening to the chatter of people around me, and finding peace in the present. For so long, I had been running from my pain, but now, I was learning to sit with it and make peace.

ᐯᐯᐯ

One particular evening, as the sun dipped below the horizon, casting a golden glow across the city, I found myself sitting by the same lake where I had once gone to cry. The wind was gentle, carrying the scent of fresh grass and earth. The sound of the water lapping against the shore was oddly comforting. It was in this peaceful place that I had come to understand one simple truth: **"The strongest hearts have the most scars."**

The betrayal that once felt like it would break me had instead become a part of my story. It had shaped me, made me stronger, and taught me things about myself I never would have learned otherwise. But I was no longer consumed by it. The pain had faded into the background, and in its place was a quiet strength I didn't even know I had.

As I sat there, I reflected on how far I had come. I had rebuilt my life—my career, my relationships, my sense of self—and now, I was finally beginning to trust again. Trust in myself. Trust in the journey. **"You can't change the past, but you can shape your future."** And I had learned how to shape mine.

ᐯᐯᐯ

A few weeks later, I was standing in front of the gallery at an exhibition. The walls were lined with breathtaking art, each piece more mesmerizing than the last. But as I looked around, I couldn't help but feel a sense of pride. This was my world now—photography, art, creativity. The interview that had seemed so daunting months ago had led me here, to a place where I could finally express myself. It was more than just an internship; it was my future unfolding right before my eyes.

I was greeted by my mentor, Maya, who was leading the exhibition. She smiled as she saw me. "Dhruv, your photos have been a big hit. People are talking about your work. You've come a long way in such a short time."

I smiled, feeling a rush of warmth in my chest. "I've learned so much, Maya. It's still overwhelming, but I'm enjoying every second of it."

She nodded, her eyes thoughtful. "That's the beauty of it. The moment you start to enjoy the process, that's when the magic happens."

Her words lingered in my mind long after we had parted ways. **Don't chase success, chase the joy of the journey. Success will follow."**

ᐅᐅᐅ

Later that evening, I was walking through the streets of Mumbai, feeling lighter than I had in years. The city had always been loud, chaotic, and full of life, but tonight, there was a quiet stillness in me that mirrored the calm of the streets. I'd learned to be at peace with the noise, to take it all in without letting it overwhelm me.

As I walked past a café, I spotted Rhea sitting at a table with her friends. She waved me over, and I joined them, grateful for her unwavering support and friendship. "Dhruv, you look like you're on top of the world!" she said with a grin. "How's everything going with the internship?"

"It's going great, actually," I replied, feeling the warmth spread across my face. "I'm learning so much. It's been a lot, but in a good way."

"I knew you'd make it," Rhea said, her eyes sparkling. "You've always had it in you. And now, you're getting the recognition you deserve."

ᐅᐅᐅ

I glanced at the group around the table, their easy laughter and relaxed conversation a reminder of how much I had grown. These were the people who had been there for me when everything seemed impossible. They had watched me fall, but more importantly, they had watched me rise. **"True friends are like stars; you don't always see them, but you know they're always there."**

The conversations flowed effortlessly, and for the first time in a long while, I felt truly at peace. There was no tension in the air, no sadness weighing me down. There was just joy—the simple joy of being present, of enjoying the company of those who mattered most.

Rhea caught my gaze and smiled. "You've come so far, Dhruv. I'm so proud of you."

Her words filled me with warmth, and I couldn't help but feel grateful. Gratitude for the people in my life, gratitude for the opportunities that had come my way, and most importantly, gratitude for the peace I had found within myself.

ᐅᐅᐅ

The following week, I received an unexpected message. It was from Naira. My heart skipped a beat, but I quickly pushed aside the old feelings that had once consumed me. **"Some people come into your life to teach you lessons, and others to make you realize how strong you truly are."**

She had apologized. Said she was sorry for everything—everything that had happened. She asked if we could meet and talk, but I didn't respond right away. Part of me wanted to, to hear her out, to see if there was closure. But another part of me knew that some conversations weren't worth having. **"Closure isn't about hearing someone's apology. It's about accepting the truth and finding peace with it."**

I took my time to think about it. And when I finally did respond, it was simple: **"I've moved on, Naira. I wish you the best, but I need to keep moving forward."**

There was no bitterness in my reply, no anger. Just calm. And in that moment, I realized something that had taken me a long time to understand. **"The most powerful thing you can do is let go." And I had finally let go.**

ᚦᚦᚦ

Days passed, and I found myself standing in front of the gallery once more, admiring the art and photographs that lined the walls. This place, this gallery, had become more than just a venue for work. It was a symbol of my growth, of everything I had overcome.

In the quiet of the evening, as I looked at the photographs, I realized that every image told a story. But those stories weren't just about what I had captured in the frame. They were about the lessons I had learned, the people who had shaped me, and the peace I had finally found. **"Sometimes, the most beautiful stories are the ones you never intended to tell."**

And in that moment, I understood that the journey wasn't over. It would never truly be over. But that was okay. **"The journey is the destination."**

As I left the gallery that night, I felt lighter, as if the weight of the world had been lifted from my shoulders. And for the first time in a long time, I truly believed it: **"The best is yet to come."**

ᚦᚦᚦ

13
The Return of Old Ghosts

The wind in Mumbai had taken on a distinct chill, signaling the approach of winter. It was that time of year when the city felt more alive—its streets bustling with the excitement of festivals, people making last-minute preparations for the new year, and the energy in the air practically crackling with the promise of something new. I had felt a shift in myself, too. After everything that had happened, I was beginning to look forward again. But sometimes, the past has a funny way of creeping back in, when you least expect it.

One evening, while I was working on a new photo project for my internship, my phone buzzed. It was a message from Arjun. I opened it, my heart instantly sinking.

"Dhruv, I need to talk to you. Can you meet me today? Something's come up."

I frowned, immediately worried. Arjun was my closest friend, the one who'd been with me through the worst of times. He'd seen me broken, picked me up, and supported me when I was barely able to stand on my own. **"True friends are the ones who lift you up when you've forgotten how to stand."**

Without hesitation, I replied, "I'll be there in an hour."

ᐁᐁᐁ

When I reached the café we had agreed to meet at, Arjun was already sitting at a corner table, looking unusually serious. I sat down across from him, my stomach in knots.

"Dhruv..." he started, his voice hesitant. "I need to tell you something about Naira."

At the mention of her name, I felt a cold shiver run down my spine. Even though I had moved on, even though I had found peace, there were still parts of me that weren't quite healed. **"The mind may forgive, but the heart takes longer."**

Arjun continued, not meeting my eyes. "She's been trying to reach you, man. I don't know how to say this, but she... she's been trying to fix things, trying to explain herself. I think she wants to meet you."

I felt my heart race, and suddenly the café around us felt like it was spinning. I was no longer in control of my emotions. For a brief moment, I had thought I was over it, that I had moved on. But the truth hit me like a wave crashing into the shore. **"Sometimes, the hardest part is**

not letting go, but learning to live without someone."

I took a deep breath, steadying myself. "Arjun, I've already moved on. I've made my peace with everything. I don't need to meet her again. It's over."

Arjun sighed, his expression a mix of concern and sadness. "I know, man. I just thought you should know. You've been through a lot, and I didn't want you to be blindsided if she reaches out again."

I nodded, appreciating his honesty. But a part of me couldn't shake the feeling of unease. **"Even when you move on, the past never completely disappears."**

ᐅᐅᐅ

I left the café feeling a mixture of frustration and confusion. I had thought I had closed that chapter of my life, but now it felt like the past was trying to break through the walls I had carefully built around it.

That night, I couldn't sleep. I tossed and turned, my mind racing with thoughts of Naira and everything that had happened. The betrayal, the pain, the heartache—it all came flooding back. **"The pain you feel today is the strength you will feel tomorrow,"** I reminded myself. But no amount of self-talk seemed to quiet the storm inside me.

The next morning, I went for a long walk, hoping the fresh air would help clear my mind. As I walked along the busy streets of Mumbai, my thoughts kept drifting back to that moment when everything had changed. To the days when I had believed in Naira, in the love we shared. **"Love doesn't hurt. Betrayal does."**

It was hard to reconcile the memories of that love with the reality of what had happened. But what I had learned, slowly but surely, was that I could no longer hold on to the past. It was time to let go completely. **"You can't start the next chapter of your life if you keep re-reading the last one."**

ᗧᗧᗧ

Later that day, I found myself sitting at the café where Arjun and I had met. But this time, I was alone, trying to make sense of everything. I needed to find closure, not in meeting Naira again, but in letting go of the last remnants of her presence in my life.

I opened my phone, and there, at the top of my messages, was Naira's name. She had sent another text. My heart thudded in my chest as I stared at the screen.

"Dhruv, I need to talk to you. I'm sorry for everything. Can we meet?"

It was exactly what Arjun had warned me about. But this time, I didn't feel anger or frustration. Instead, I felt a deep sense of peace. I had come so far, and I knew that meeting Naira wouldn't change anything. **"Some people come into your life for a reason. Others just come to teach you a lesson."**

I didn't respond to her message. I simply put my phone down and took a deep breath, letting the silence fill the space around me. **"Letting go doesn't mean giving up. It means moving forward."**

❧❧❧

The next few days passed in a blur. I focused more on my photography and spent time with friends, allowing myself to heal further. It wasn't that I had completely forgotten Naira or the pain of the past. But I had come to a point where I no longer needed her apology to feel whole again.

"Forgiveness is not for the person who wronged you. It's for your peace of mind."

The day came when I finally received an email from the gallery. They had offered me a full-time position as a junior photographer, which meant I could leave my part-time job and focus completely on my passion. **"Opportunities don't come by every day, Dhruv,"** Maya had said when she told me the good news. **"Take it and make the most of it."**

I couldn't believe it. I had worked so hard to get here, and now, the universe was rewarding me. For a moment, I felt like everything had fallen into place. **"Success is not the key to happiness. Happiness is the key to success."**

❧❧❧

And so, I moved forward. Slowly, but surely, my life began to take on new meaning. I stopped looking back and focused on what lay ahead. I had learned to trust myself, to believe in my journey, and to accept that not all things were meant to last forever.

I never responded to Naira's messages. She had been a part of my story, but she no longer defined it. **"The people who hurt you are not worth your time. You have a future to look forward to."**

In the end, it wasn't about the closure I thought I needed. It was about creating a future filled with peace, passion, and the people who truly mattered. And I had found that in myself.

"The best revenge is to live a happy life."

ᚦᚦᚦ

The days following the message from Naira had felt oddly heavy, as if the past was trying to claw its way back into my life. No matter how hard I tried to ignore it, the emotional waves would hit me at unexpected times. **"Some scars you can't see, but you feel them,"** and that was how I felt—every emotion I had buried under the surface began to resurface slowly, like water breaking through cracks in a dam.

As I sat in my room, reviewing photographs for the exhibition, my thoughts kept drifting back to the times when everything seemed perfect. When I was so sure that love could be the answer to all my problems, when I believed that the future was built on shared dreams and promises. But now, every time I thought of Naira, it felt like that love was a distant memory, a part of a past I was no longer sure I wanted to be a part of. **"We loved with**

a love that was more than love," but love alone wasn't enough when trust was broken.

The message still sat there in my inbox, taunting me. **"Why does it always feel like the things we try to forget are the things that come back to haunt us?"** But I had already made my decision—there was no room for the past in my present. There was no place for the things I couldn't change.

ᐁᐁᐁ

Over the next few days, I began noticing changes in myself. It wasn't that I had forgotten the pain, or that the betrayal no longer stung. But I was learning how to live with it. **"Healing doesn't mean the pain goes away, it means you learn to live with it."** And for the first time in months, I started to see the light again. I wasn't running from the pain. I was facing it head-on, accepting that it would always be a part of me, but it didn't define me anymore.

I found myself spending more time with Rhea and the others, reconnecting with the people who truly understood me. Rhea had been such a constant support throughout this whole ordeal, and I couldn't have asked for a better friend. We laughed together, talked about everything and nothing, and I started feeling like myself again.

One evening, as we sat at a café near the beach, she turned to me with a serious expression.

"Dhruv, you're different now. I can see it. It's like you've found a new strength in yourself," she said, her voice soft.

I smiled, but it wasn't a sad smile anymore. It was genuine. "I guess I have. It's not easy, but I'm getting there."

"Are you still thinking about her?" Rhea asked, her tone gentle, but I could tell she knew how much it still hurt me.

I hesitated for a moment before responding, **"I don't know if I'm thinking about her, or if I'm just thinking about the person I used to be when I was with her. I guess there's a difference."**

Rhea nodded, understanding more than I expected. **"We are all a collection of who we used to be and who we choose to become. But you, Dhruv, you've chosen to become someone who doesn't let his past decide his future."**

I laughed softly at her words. **"You know, sometimes I think you give me more credit than I deserve."**

"I'm just telling the truth," she said, smiling back. "You're stronger than you know. And you're finally living for yourself. It's about time."

ϼϼϼ

Over the next few weeks, I focused more on my photography, diving into projects that excited me, pushing myself further than I ever had before. **"The best way to**

predict the future is to create it," and that's exactly what I was doing. With every photograph I clicked, I felt a sense of freedom, of control, of building something that was uniquely mine.

I spent time developing a portfolio that would get me noticed, and it wasn't long before my work began to gain attention. A few of my photos were picked up by well-known magazines, and soon, I was being invited to showcase my work at a professional exhibition. The validation felt good, but what was even better was the feeling that I had reclaimed something precious—myself.

One evening, after a particularly exhausting but rewarding day, I sat in my apartment, looking through the new photos I had taken. The harsh, fluorescent light of the room was a stark contrast to the soft, golden glow of the sunset I had captured in my latest piece. As I stared at the image, something inside me clicked. I finally understood what my journey had been about: it wasn't about erasing the past, or trying to forget the betrayal. It was about **embracing the pain and turning it into something beautiful.** Like a photograph—capturing a moment, preserving it, and turning it into art.

ppp

It was around this time that I received another message from Naira. This time, it wasn't just a simple text. She had written a long, heartfelt letter, apologizing for everything that had happened between us. She expressed regret for her actions and asked me to forgive her. She told me that she had made a mistake and that she had been lost, but that she was finally starting to understand the consequences of her choices.

I read the letter in silence, my emotions swirling inside me. I knew that, for her, this letter might have been her attempt at closure, but for me, it didn't change anything. I had already found my own peace, and I no longer needed her apology to move on. **"Forgiveness isn't about letting the other person off the hook. It's about freeing yourself from the weight of the past."**

I put the phone down, taking a deep breath. **"The hardest part of healing is realizing that not everything will have the closure you expect, and that's okay."**

ᐅᐅᐅ

The day of the exhibition arrived, and as I stood in front of my work, I felt a deep sense of pride. The crowd around me admired the pieces, complimenting my work, but what made me feel truly accomplished was the realization that I had done this for myself. **"You don't find yourself by going out there. You find yourself by looking inward."**

Rhea came up to me, her face glowing with excitement. "Dhruv, this is amazing! You've really made it. I'm so proud of you!"

I smiled at her, grateful for everything she had done for me. "Thank you, Rhea. I couldn't have done this without your support."

She laughed. "You did the hard work. I just cheered you on."

But what she didn't know was that her support had been my anchor when everything else felt like it was falling apart. **"In the end, the people who stay with you during your darkest times are the ones who make you shine brightest."**

As the night wore on, I stood back and watched the crowd admiring my work, the compliments flowing in, the sense of accomplishment washing over me. But even more than the accolades, I felt something deeper—a sense of peace, a knowing that I had taken control of my life again. **"You are the author of your own story. Don't let anyone else hold the pen."**

And just like that, in the midst of the applause and the admiration, I finally understood that I wasn't defined by the betrayal, by the heartbreak, or by the people who had come and gone. I was defined by how I rose from it, how I learned to live again, how I built something new from the ruins.

"The pain you experience today will make you stronger tomorrow. It will lead you to the version of yourself that you were always meant to become."

ᗰᗰᗰ

14
The New Beginning

It was a quiet evening when I sat by my window, watching the vibrant Mumbai city lights flicker like fireflies in the distance. The city that had once felt so overwhelming to me now seemed like a place of endless possibilities, full of stories waiting to be written. For the first time in months, I felt at peace.

"Sometimes, you have to step back and look at the bigger picture. Life moves on, and so do you." That was what I had learned over the past year—nothing is permanent, and change, no matter how painful, brings new opportunities.

I had grown. I had healed. But most importantly, I had found my strength again.

ᗡᗡᗡ

The exhibition was behind me, and with it came a wave of new projects and opportunities. My photos were now being showcased in several high-end galleries across the city. I was doing interviews with photographers who I had once looked up to. My name was slowly becoming known in the world I had always dreamed of. I had started living my dream, not as an escape from the past, but as a result of it.

Rhea had always believed in me, even when I couldn't believe in myself. **"You always find your way back to yourself,"** she said, and now, I could finally see it. I wasn't just a boy who had been betrayed; I was a man who had risen from the ashes, stronger and more determined than ever.

But as life began to move forward, something I had feared for a while happened—Naira tried to reach out again.

It was late one night when my phone buzzed with an unfamiliar number. I answered it, and a voice I hadn't heard in so long came through the receiver.

"Dhruv... it's me. Naira."

I froze for a moment, but I had learned long ago not to react impulsively. **"You don't have to give power to things that no longer affect you,"** I thought to myself as I took a deep breath.

Her voice was soft, almost tentative, as if unsure of how to start. "I... I don't expect you to forgive me or to even want to talk to me. But I wanted to say that I'm sorry. For everything. I never meant to hurt you, and I regret every single thing that happened between us."

I closed my eyes, the weight of her words sinking in. But I didn't feel the same anger, the same hurt that I once had. **"Forgiveness is a gift you give yourself."** It wasn't about her anymore; it was about me letting go of a past that had once defined me.

"I appreciate your apology, Naira," I said calmly, my voice steady. "But I'm not the same person anymore. I've learned to live without the past, and I need to keep moving forward. I'm sorry, but I can't go back."

There was silence on the other end, and I could almost hear her taking in what I had said. Finally, she spoke, her voice shaky. "I understand, Dhruv. And I'm sorry for everything."

I hung up the phone, my mind swirling with mixed emotions. **"It's not about what the other person did. It's about what you choose to do with what you have left."** And I had chosen peace.

▷▷▷

The next few weeks passed in a blur of photographs, exhibitions, and interviews. Every moment felt like a gift I had given myself after years of pain. But there were moments—quiet, solitary moments—when I would reflect on everything that had happened. I would think about the boy I had been and the man I had become. **"You never know how strong you are until being strong is your only choice."**

My relationship with my family had also evolved. My mumma and papa, after initially scolding me for my choices, had begun to understand that my passion for photography wasn't just a phase. They had begun to support me, even if they didn't fully understand it. And didi, well, she was always there, always reminding me to take a step back and breathe, always pushing me forward when I wanted to give up.

"I'm proud of you, Dhruv," didi said one evening, as we sat together at home. "You've come so far. From being lost in your own grief to finding a new version of yourself. I hope you know how much you've grown."

I smiled, looking at her with gratitude. "I couldn't have done it without you."

ᐅᐅᐅ

But despite the newfound peace I had, there was still one last piece to the puzzle.

It was at a gallery opening one evening that I bumped into Arjun. He had been my rock throughout everything, always ready with a word of encouragement or a quiet listening ear when I needed it most. And I realized that while Naira and everything else had been a chapter in my life, it was the friendships I had that had really shaped who I had become.

Arjun looked at me as we shared a drink, his eyes full of pride. "I knew you had it in you. You're unstoppable now, Dhruv."

I laughed, shaking my head. "I don't know about that, man. But I've learned that the hardest battles teach you the most."

"Exactly. And look where you are now." Arjun smiled, raising his glass. "To the future."

We clinked our glasses together, the sound a small but powerful reminder of how far I had come.

ϷϷϷ

The following months were filled with new challenges, new beginnings, and new stories waiting to be told. As I worked on a new photo book project, I started reflecting on my journey more deeply. There was a part of me that wanted to write about it, to capture everything in words. But I realized that sometimes the most powerful stories are the ones that are told through silence, through the images that speak louder than words ever could.

"We all have a story. But the most important part is not how we start it, but how we finish it." I had come a long way, from the boy who had believed in love to the man who understood its complexities. From the heartbroken soul who had been betrayed to the one who had learned the value of self-love and forgiveness.

As I sat in front of my camera one evening, preparing for yet another shoot, I understood what the next chapter of my life would be. It wouldn't be defined by my past mistakes or the people who had hurt me. It would be defined by the person I had become—the artist, the man who had learned to rebuild from the wreckage.

I was no longer just a product of my circumstances. I was the architect of my future.

ᗷᗷᗷ

And as I clicked the shutter, capturing another moment in time, I knew that this was only the beginning. The future, my future, was wide open. **"The best is yet to come."**

ᗷᗷᗷ

15
The Road Ahead & The Final Goodbye.

As I stood on the rooftop of my apartment building, watching the sun dip beneath the horizon, I felt a sense of finality. The city was alive with lights, the hum of traffic in the distance blending with the soft whisper of the evening breeze. It was one of those rare moments when everything felt still, when time seemed to stretch out endlessly before me. **"The past is never really gone. It's the lessons you carry with you that shape who you are."**

This was it—the end of one journey, but not the end of my story. The chapters that had once felt like a never-ending loop of pain, betrayal, and confusion had slowly faded, leaving behind a person I could finally be proud of. A person who had learned the value of strength, of resilience, and most importantly, of self-love.

As I reflected on everything that had happened—the heartbreak, the betrayal, the long nights of feeling lost—it struck me how much I had changed. I had spent so many months thinking I was broken, unable to repair the damage done to me. But the truth was, the cracks in my heart had only allowed the light to come in. **"Sometimes you have to go through the worst to get to the best."**

I had learned that the greatest healing didn't come from erasing the past. It came from understanding it, embracing it, and using it to fuel my future. The person who had fallen in love with Naira, who had believed in the purity of love, was still there, but he was wiser now. He knew that love, while beautiful, wasn't the answer to everything. He knew that sometimes, you had to let go of things—people, places, memories—so that you could grow into the person you were meant to be.

ᗑᗑᗑ

Rhea had called me that morning, reminding me that there was a photography event at the gallery later that evening. I had almost forgotten about it, consumed with my own thoughts, but I was glad she had reminded me. This was my world now—the world I had worked so hard to build. I had made a name for myself, and the journey had just begun.

ᗑᗑᗑ

The gallery was buzzing with energy as I walked in. People were admiring the art, discussing their favorite pieces, and engaging in conversations about photography and life. I could feel the excitement in the air, and for the first time in a long time, I didn't feel out of place.

Rhea was already there, standing near one of the walls, her eyes scanning the crowd. When she saw me, she flashed a bright smile and waved me over.

"Dhruv!" she exclaimed. "You look amazing tonight!"

I chuckled, adjusting the collar of my shirt. "Thanks, Rhea. It feels good to be here, you know? Like, this is where I'm meant to be."

She raised an eyebrow. "I thought you were already doing great. What do you mean, 'meant to be'?"

I looked at her, feeling a sense of clarity I hadn't felt in years. "I mean, all of this—the photography, the exhibitions, the recognition—it's not just about the work. It's about me finding my purpose again. After everything that happened, I couldn't see it. But now, I finally understand."

Rhea nodded, her eyes full of understanding. **"Life has a funny way of showing you the path when you least expect it. But you've always had it in you, Dhruv. You just had to see it for yourself."**

I smiled, grateful for her unwavering support. "I don't know what I would've done without you."

ᗡᗡᗡ

As the evening unfolded, I stood back and observed the interactions around me. People discussing the pieces, photographers sharing tips and experiences. The world I had once only dreamed of was now my reality, and for the first time, I could see it clearly. I had worked hard to get here, and every step had been worth it.

My phone buzzed in my pocket, pulling me from my thoughts. I pulled it out to see a message from Arjun: **"The road ahead is long, but you're ready for it. You've already made it further than most ever will."**

I smiled at the message. Arjun had been there for me from the beginning, and his words always had a way of grounding me.

ᐅᐅᐅ

Later that night, as I left the gallery, the city streets felt like a familiar friend. The noise, the lights, the constant movement—it had all once overwhelmed me, but now it felt like home. I had embraced the chaos of the city, the ups and downs, the ebbs and flows, and I had found my rhythm in it.

I knew that this was just the beginning of something much bigger. There would be new challenges, new opportunities, and of course, new moments of doubt. But now, I knew that I was strong enough to face whatever came my way. **"Strength doesn't come from what you can do. It comes from overcoming the things you once thought you couldn't."**

ᐅᐅᐅ

As I walked along the street, the cool night air brushing against my skin, I felt the weight of the past lift off my shoulders. The betrayal, the heartbreak—it had all shaped me, but it didn't define me. I was Dhruv, the photographer, the dreamer, the man who had learned to turn his pain into something beautiful. **"Your story is yours to write. Don't let anyone else hold the pen."**

And in that moment, I understood that the road ahead wasn't just about success or recognition. It was about growth. About living my truth. About becoming the person I was always meant to be.

I didn't need to look back anymore, because I knew that the best was yet to come. **"The future belongs to those who believe in the beauty of their dreams."**

ᏢᏢᏢ

The evening felt different, quieter, as if the world itself had paused, holding its breath. I stood in the center of my room, surrounded by the remnants of a past I was trying to let go of. On the floor lay the pile of photographs, letters, and little trinkets from my time with Naira. Each one a memory that had once been precious but had now become a weight I no longer wanted to carry.

It had taken me months to get to this moment—the moment when I could finally part with everything that had held me hostage. The betrayal, the hurt, the countless nights spent wondering if she had ever truly loved me—they all lingered in these images, in these pieces of paper that carried the weight of broken promises.

But now, standing in front of the small fire I had lit in a metal container, I felt a sense of closure I hadn't thought possible. The flames danced in the dim light, flickering and crackling as they consumed the past, bit by bit. One by one, the photographs curled and blackened, the ink on the letters smudging into oblivion. It was as if I were erasing her from my life completely, burying the parts of her that had once meant everything to me.

ϷϷϷ

I knelt beside the fire, holding the last photograph of her in my hands. I looked at her face—her smile, her eyes, the way she had looked at me back when we were happy, before everything fell apart. I thought back to the days when I believed in us, when I had no idea what was coming.

For a brief moment, I felt a pang of sadness, a flicker of the love that had once been. But I didn't let it consume me. "It's not about forgetting. It's about accepting." I whispered the words to myself, the lesson I had learned so painfully over the months.

I held her photo up to the flame, staring at it one last time.

Fate's regret," I whispered, almost as if I were saying it to her, to myself, to the world. **"I wish we had never met."**

The words echoed in my mind, not because I hated her or because I was angry anymore. It was because, in that moment, I realized that meeting her had changed me. It had hurt me in ways I could never have imagined, but it had also taught me lessons I would carry with me forever. I had learned that life wasn't always kind, and that sometimes, people come into your life for reasons you don't understand.

But no matter how much it hurt, I had learned to stand on my own again. **"The pain you feel today is the strength you'll feel tomorrow."**

As the photograph burned to ash, I watched as the last remnants of the past were consumed by the flames. There would be no more letters, no more photographs to remind me of what I had lost. Just a memory, fading into nothing, leaving behind the lessons learned.

I stood up, taking a deep breath, feeling the weight in my chest finally begin to lift. It wasn't easy to let go, but sometimes, it was the only way to move forward. **"Sometimes the only way to move forward is to leave the past behind."**

ᖇᖇᖇ

The fire burned out, leaving only the scent of smoke in the air. I knew that I was finally free. Free from the memories, the pain, and the person who had once been everything to me but now felt like a ghost of the past.

As I left the room and closed the door behind me, I looked out the window at the city below. The lights twinkled like a thousand possibilities, and for the first time in a long time, I felt at peace with myself. I wasn't the same person who had fallen in love with Naira. I wasn't the boy who had been betrayed. I was Dhruv—the man who had learned to rise from the ashes.

"Don't be afraid of moving forward. You never know what beautiful things are waiting ahead."

ᐅᐅᐅ

Life had taught me a lot during the past year. It had been hard, it had been painful, but it had also been beautiful in its own way. I had learned that I was stronger than I thought, that I could endure more than I had ever imagined. And most importantly, I had learned that happiness wasn't something you could find in someone else—it was something that came from within.

I had lost something precious, yes, but in return, I had gained something far more valuable: a sense of self, a renewed passion for life, and a future that was mine to shape.

As I stood in the middle of the room, looking out at the city, I made a silent promise to myself: **"I will live for me now."**

ᐅᐅᐅ

And with that, I took one last look at the city before walking out the door. There was no more looking back. Only forward. The past had given me the lessons I needed, and now it was time for me to step into the future with my head held high.

ᚦᚦᚦ

"Sometimes you have to go through the worst to get to the best."

"The past is never really gone. It's the lessons you carry with you that shape who you are."

"Forgiveness is a gift you give yourself."

161

"Strength doesn't come from what you can do. It comes from overcoming the things you once thought you couldn't."

"Your story is yours to write. Don't let anyone else hold the pen."

"The future belongs to those who believe in the beauty
of their dreams."

"It's not about forgetting. It's about accepting."

169

"Sometimes the only way to move forward is to leave the past behind."

"The pain you feel today is the strength you'll feel tomorrow."

173

"Don't be afraid of moving forward. You never know what beautiful things are waiting ahead."

www.ingramcontent.com/pod-product-compliance
Lightning Source LLC
Chambersburg PA
CBHW031042160726
47991CB00005B/1998